Amber
Ambrosia

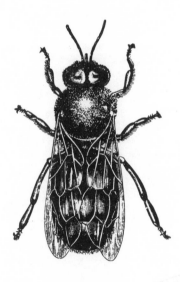

RAE BRIDGE

Great Plains Publications
420 – 70 Arthur Street
Winnipeg, MB R3B 1G7
www.greatplains.mb.ca

Great Plains Publications gratefully acknowledges the financial support provided for its publishing program by the Government of Canada through the Book Publishing Industry Development Program (BPIDP); the Canada Council for the Arts; as well as the Manitoba Department of Culture, Heritage and Tourism; and the Manitoba Arts Council.

Design & Typography by Relish Design Studios Ltd.
Printed in Canada by Friesens
Text and illustrations at chapters' beginning © 2007 Rae Bridgman.

The passage by Virgil is reprinted with grateful acknowledgement to Hackett Publishing Company, Inc. from *Georgics* by Virgil, translated by Kristine Chew. Copyright 2002 by Hackett Publishing Company, Inc. Reprinted by permission of Hackett Publishing Company, Inc. All rights reserved.

The passage from Aristotle's *Historia Animalium* is reprinted with grateful acknowledgement to Oxford University Press. By permission of Oxford University Press, 23 words *Historia Animalium* translated by D'Arcy W. Thompson from *History of Animals: Oxford Translation of Aristotle* by Aristotle edited by Ross, W.D. (2005). Free permission.

The passage from Emily Dickinson's poem is reprinted with grateful acknowledgement to the Trustees of Amherst College from *The Poems of Emily Dickinson*, Thomas H. Johnston, Ed., Cambridge, Mass. The Belknap Press of Harvard University Press copyright 1951, 1955, 1979, 1983 by the President and Fellows of Harvard College.

This is a work of fiction. Names, characters, places and incidents are used fictitiously or are the product of the author's imagination. Any resemblance to actual persons, living or dead, is entirely coincidental.

My thanks to Carol Steer for her perennial enthusiasm and help with the Latin translations at the beginning of each chapter.

CANADIAN CATALOGUING IN PUBLICATION DATA

Main entry under title:
Bridgman, Rae
Amber ambrosia / Rae Bridgman.

(The serpent's chain)
ISBN 978-1-894283-73-1

I. Title II. Series: Bridgman, Rae. Serpent's chain.
PS8603.R528A43 2007   jC813'.6   C2007-900425-3

AMBER
AMBROSIA

ORITUR LECTOR, PRAETERIT UMBRA.
ORITUR NUMQUAM LUNA, OCCIDIT NUMQUAM SOL.
HAEC FABULA NE SIT FICTA METUO VERE.
O NATI, FABULA NARRAT NIHIL NISI VERA.
THE READER AWAKES, A SHADOW PASSES BY.
THE MOON NEVER RISES, THE SUN NEVER SETS.
THIS TALE, I FEAR, IS VERILY A LIE.
O CHILDREN, WHAT IT TELLS IS NOTHING BUT THE TRUTH.

So great is their love of flowers
And the glory of making honey.
　　　　– Virgil's *Georgics* IV, 'The Race of Bees'

…honey is distilled from dew, and is deposited chiefly at the risings
of the constellations or when a rainbow is in the sky…
　　　　– Aristotle's *Historia Animalium* V. 22

To make a prairie it takes a clover and one bee,—
One clover, and a bee,
And revery.
The revery alone will do
If bees are few.
　　　　– Emily Dickinson

Contents

PROLOGUE

The winds of change...

SCELESTARUM INSIDIARUM
ET MALORUM CONSILIORUM
INOPIA NULLA, MALE, EST.
OF WICKED PLOTS AND EVIL PLANS
THERE IS NO DEARTH, UNFORTUNATELY.

A dusty clock on the wall ticked. It was eleven forty-five. Dangling from a twisted cord, one light bulb cast a misshapen circle of light around a red-haired man sitting at a wooden table. Stuffed furniture draped in sheets and a large chandelier strung with cobwebs added to the general gloom of the room. The man hunched over a bowl of steaming, pale yellow soup.

A black-haired woman stood motionless by the window, looking down the full length of the street. Her gaze paused at a leafless elm tree shrouded in cankerworm webs. Moonlight grazed her face—a face with dark eyes, high cheekbones and parchment skin. Then clouds cloaked the moon, and her face was cast into shadow.

The man bent his head and took a sip of the soup.

The woman turned away from the window and sat down at the table. She watched the man silently, while her fingers fidgeted with the corner of a newspaper on the table. Finally, she pushed the paper towards him.

The man thrust the newspaper away and the sound of ripping paper slashed the room's silence. The picture of a woman on the front page—a woman with white, fluffy hair and thick glasses—was torn in half.

"The boy is not interes-s-sted," the man said, and he bent his head to take another spoonful of soup. He swallowed and cleared his throat. "We had not counted on that medallion protecting its owner s-s-o."

"Forget about the boy," said the woman in a hoarse voice. "You are foolish if you think they won't find you. It's not safe here." Ignoring the rip in the paper, she pointed to the headlines. "Look what they're saying in *The Daily Magezine*."

BRIMSTONE SNAKES LONG-LOST PORTAL
SNAKE IN THE GRASS CAPTURED

"*Snake in the Grass?* Now who could that be?" said the man, sounding pleased. He put his spoon down and squinted at the front page in the dim light. He began to read aloud:

> *Two children discovered the Brimstone Snakes monument is a long-lost gate to the caves of Narcisse, and the mystery of who has been behind the murder of the snakes of Narcisse drew to a close last night. Authorities have also at long-last apprehended the notorious rogue known as the Snake in the Grass.*

"*Notorious-s-s?*" said the man. "How flattering."

"Won't they be suspicious about the glass vial you were carrying and that dead bee in the film canister?" asked the woman.

"A harmless little bee…and the vile vial was empty anyway," said the man, waving his hand dismissively as he laughed at his own pun. "We are only helping others-s-s do what they wish. What greater good is there? Dreams-s-s make us-s-s human. Without dreams, we would be nothing. Together, we can help others achieve their dreams—so s-s-simple, isn't it? You'll join us-s-s this time, won't you?"

The woman did not reply, but her eyes glittered.

The man smiled and blew her a kiss. He flicked to the end of the article:

> *...tight security around the Brimstone Snakes and the Narcisse caves will continue to be enforced.*

> *According to one government source, who spoke on condition of anonymity, the Firecatchers suspect Rufus Crookshank may be one link—*

Here the man stopped, his voice quivering—either from fear or excitement, or both.

The woman stiffened. "Well?"

> *—the Firecatchers suspect Rufus Crookshank may be one link in an organization known as The Serpent's Chain.*

"Yes!" The woman took a deep breath, and laughed. "The Serpent's Chain has returned!" she said.

The man held up the bowl of soup.

"Here's to our health. Cheers-s-s, s-s-sweet love."

He brought the bowl to his lips and slurped the last of the soup, which was now stone cold.

İ Licences, Permits and Fines

Popcorn clouds danced across the periwinkle sky.

O FUGAX FAMA MOBILIS
IN TUA LUCE APRICEM.
O FAME, FICKLE AND FLEETING,
YET, LET ME BASK IN YOUR LIGHT.

Wil could not remember a time when he had been happier, even though, truth be known, he was a little nervous about having to register his snake Esme at the Secretariat on the Status of Magical Creatures—or S.S.M.C., for short. He clutched Esme's cage and hurried to keep up with his old friend Mr. Bertram and his cousin Sophie.

It was a brilliant blue and white morning; popcorn clouds danced across the periwinkle sky and glistening silk threads from the cankerworms—long threads tossed by the wind—jewelled the elm trees in the sunlight.

The cankerworms nibbled—no, devoured—the leaves (until nothing was left of them but green lace), and it was hard to walk without bumping into the creatures as they hung suspended from the trees like tiny, writhing Egyptian mummies. Suddenly, it seemed they were everywhere—even inside the house. Aunt Violet had screeched when one dangled from her eyeglasses and dropped right onto her toast. Sophie had laughed so hard she almost couldn't stop; and the frames of her eyeglasses had turned from bubblegum pink to fluorescent orange polka dots. But now—when Wil and Sophie had to miss school in order to register Esme—all of MiddleGate seemed to have been transformed into a royal city robed in the finest silver and gold cankerworm silks.

For they were heroes.

Had he and Sophie not captured a known criminal, Rufus Crookshank, who had been masquerading as the librarian Miss Heese? Had they not saved thousands and thousands of the snakes at Narcisse from being murdered by Crookshank? Had his snake Esme not come to his rescue? Had he not, for a brief time, understood the deadly power of that ancient game snapdragon—a game of wits between shadows?

❖❖❖❖❖❖

From a distance, the Secretariat looked like any other large government building. Up close, though, stone snakes slithered across its walls under the watchful gaze of stone bald eagles sitting on top of the columns. Stone fishes, so life-like Wil thought they would jump if he touched them, taunted a stone beaver with a large, flat paddle tail. The massive stone bison directly above the door glared down on all who entered, while stone peacocks strutted beside tall, muscular stone women and men dressed in togas and carrying sheaves of wheat.

Wil was so busy gawking at all the sculptures that he stumbled on his way up the Secretariat stairs.

"Wil, be careful," said Mr. Bertram, "or you'll drop Esme."

The door to Esme's cage swung open and Wil managed to close it just in time before she could escape.

"Do you want me to take the cage for you?" asked Mr. Bertram.

"No, that's okay," said Wil, reluctantly leaving ideas of fame and glory behind. Clutching Esme's cage, he mounted the stairs to the Secretariat, following on the heels of Mr. Bertram and Sophie, who was still limping from having fallen on the rocks at Narcisse.

The guard at the front desk appeared not to notice they were standing at the door, and Wil had a sudden and awful thought. What if they take Esme away because they think I can't take proper care of her?

Only after Mr. Bertram knocked loudly on the door, did the guard look up from the *Burning Heart* magazine she was reading. Then the door swung open noiselessly and they stepped into the large foyer of the Secretariat.

Inside was as sumptuous as outside. Above their heads, a stone dog grinned down at them from an ornate column. By now, though, Wil was used to feeling as if he were always being watched by stone sculptures. Gruffud's Academy for the Magical Arts, where he and his cousin Sophie attended school, was crammed with stone carvings. A creature with four horns, yawning nostrils and sharp, pointed teeth— it was stone-frozen in the act of ripping a page out of a book—had stared at him during Mage Adderson's whole numeristics exam in Stone Hall, as though to say, *Try and stop me.* Wil had been happy to escape its baleful gaze at exam's end.

Wil half expected this stone dog to turn and wag its tail—but it was not alive…unlike Portia and Portius, the two-faced stone Gatekeeper at Gruffud's Academy.

The guard drawled in a bored voice, "May I help you?" as though she could hardly wait to return to the *Burning Heart* magazine she'd been reading.

Wil's heart was pounding loudly. He wished Aunt Rue had been able to come with them, but she had had to leave early for the Secretariat. Another emergency meeting. There had been lots of emergency meetings recently. But Aunt Rue wasn't allowed to tell anyone about the meetings; they were top-secret.

Sophie must have been as nervous as he was, because she was squirming and dancing from foot to foot.

The woman behind the desk glanced at her suspiciously.

Sophie blurted, "May I please use the washroom?"

"Washrooms are down the hall to your right," said the woman, "but make sure you return here immediately. Visitors aren't allowed to wander through the building; things have been tightening up with everything that's going on."

Mr. Bertram cleared his throat and gestured to the cage in Wil's arms. "Ah, we're here to register a magical creature, a snake."

"Oh," said the woman, with no apparent interest in the subject. "First floor, down the hall to the left, at the end," she said. "Look for the sign that says *Licences, Permits and Fines.*" She turned back to her *Burning Heart* magazine with its cover picture of a large crystal ball and pink headlines

MAKE A FORTUNE SELLING FORTUNES!

❖❖❖❖❖❖

The clerk standing behind the tall counter in the *Office of Licences, Permits and Fines* looked forbidding. *Mrs. Margaret Clop* read her name tag.

"Name of Creature?" asked Mrs. Clop, and she pulled out a ream of papers from underneath the counter along with a pen.

Wil looked at the papers and his heart sank. He hadn't thought registration would be so complicated and he wondered if everyone who worked at the Secretariat was always so grumpy.

"The creature does have a name, doesn't it? If not, we'll have to assign one," said Mrs. Clop.

"No…yes…I mean, she's got a name," said Wil.

"Well, what is it?" asked Mrs. Clop. "Is it a secret?" Without waiting for Wil to answer, she continued, "We can assign another name, but we'll have to have the secret one on file."

"No, it's not a secret," said Wil. "It's Esme. *E-s-m-e.*"

"Name of Applicant please?"

"Name of what?" asked Wil, feeling his face flush.

"She means—" Mr. Bertram began to interject.

"I'm sorry," said Mrs. Clop firmly. "Only the Applicant himself may fill out the Registration Application. This legal document will have to signed by the Applicant."

"Name of Applicant…*your* name," said Mrs. Clop, staring at Wil as if he were thick.

"Oh, *my* name. My name is Wil, I mean, William Wychwood," said Wil, and Mr. Bertram gave him an encouraging look.

"How do you spell that?" asked the clerk.

As Wil began to spell his name, another clerk bustled to the counter—Mrs. *Lucy Flyboottom.* "Why, Maggie, you must know who this boy is," she exclaimed. "He's a hero! William Wychwood and his cousin, Sophie Isidor—you remember Rue Isidor's niece? Rue Isidor—works in our Endangered Insects division. They're the ones who saved the snakes of Narcisse."

"Oh really, Lucy," said Mrs. Clop, looking thoroughly unimpressed. "Who doesn't know the Isidor family?" She sniffed and looked down at Wil. "Saving snakes is one thing; however, you can't register a magical creature without completing the Form—in triplicate… infamous or not."

"We might as well let bygones be bygones. If you're not going to ask for his autograph, I am," said Mrs. Flyboottom, ignoring Mrs. Clop's ill humour. "I've got *The Daily Magezine* article right here. William Wychwood, would you be so kind as to sign across the nose of that nasty Rufus Crookshank. Imagine *The Snake in the Grass* right here in MiddleGate!"

Feeling self-conscious, Wil set Esme's cage down on the counter. Under Mrs. Flyboottom's beaming smile, he wrote his name smack in the middle of Rufus Crookshank's nose and across his left eye.

"There, done," he said, handing back the paper with an embarrassed smile.

"And someday I'll be able to say, *To think I knew him when he was a little boy,*" said Mrs. Flyboottom, brandishing the front page of the newspaper in front of Mrs. Clop. "William Wychwood will be famous some day and here's his autograph. What am I saying? He's famous now. Without him—and his snake Esme—who knows what would have happened to the snakes of Narcisse!"

"Thank you, Lucy. Now we've got that little piece of business taken care of, may we finish the Application?" snapped Mrs. Clop, clearly annoyed at her co-worker's gushing enthusiasm. "Date of birth please," she said to Wil.

"I don't know."

"What do you mean, you don't know?" asked Mrs. Clop with a withering look.

"Well, she's probably almost two years old," said Wil, trying desperately to remember when Mr. Bertram had given him the wriggling, little snake he had immediately named Esme.

"Not the snake," said Mrs. Clop, her voice rising. "You...*your* date of birth. You must be at least ten years old in order to obtain a licence for a snake."

ii The Middle of Nowhere

...without noticing the small sign posted on the door.

INTERDUM NOVIORES SERMONES AUSCULTAS IN LATRINA.
SOMETIMES YOU OVERHEAR INTERESTING
CONVERSATIONS IN A WASHROOM.

Sophie peeped into the washroom. It was empty. A fancy mirror—marbled silver and black, and engraved with a large and spectacular peacock—filled one entire wall of the room. Under the watchful eyes of the peacock, she darted into the last stall, not noticing the small sign posted on the door.

She locked the door and sat down with great relief. A moment later, she was about to flush the toilet when she heard someone come in.

"There's no one in here, is there?" said a woman with a husky voice, the voice of an older woman.

There was a small silence before the other woman answered in a much younger, lilting voice. "No, I don't think so."

Sophie ducked her head down and peeked under the door of the stall. She could see a pair of black spiky shoes with a shiny silver buckle. Their owner was standing by one of the sinks in front of the peacock mirror. A tap turned on and water splashed.

"Don't know what the Secretariat is going to do," said the older woman. "We can't have it leaking to the newspapers."

"Seems like we're constantly trying to keep a lid on bad news, doesn't it?" said the younger woman.

"...what I know...precious honey...*magykalis*...*apiponis destructor*," said the older woman.

With the water running, Sophie had difficulty hearing exactly what was being said. Sneaking snake, she cursed silently. What is an *apiponis destructor?* she thought, wishing she hadn't been forced to eavesdrop. But it was far too late to say anything now. *Magykalis* must mean something magical. But what did an *apiponis destructor* have to do with honey? Whatever an *apiponis destructor* was, it didn't sound good.

Her feeling of foreboding grew when she saw a small note scrawled on the washroom wall.

The
End
Is
Nigh

Stop it, Sophie, she thought. You're getting as gloomy as Aunt Violet with all her predictions.

The tap turned off suddenly.

"They say if it falls into the wrong hands," said the younger woman, "it could threaten national security."

National security. Sophie's breath quickened. That sounded big and it sounded dangerous. As Sophie leaned forward to hear more, she inadvertently brushed against the handle of the toilet.

A great whoosh from the toilet echoed in the bathroom and Sophie almost squealed from fright.

"Someone's in here," said the older woman.

Sophie's stomach lurched.

"Don't worry," said the younger woman. "Toilet...fixing...sign... Out of Order."

"Oh, right," said the older woman.

Sophie heaved a sigh of relief. She peered through the crack in the door. There was an older, black-haired woman crimping her hair and a younger woman applying mascara to her eyelashes. The older woman took out a bottle and sprayed her neck with what must have been a fountain of perfume.

The overwhelming smell of pungent lavender filled the bathroom, and Sophie had the irresistible urge to sneeze loudly. She held her nose tightly and coughed; fortunately, the still-flushing toilet drowned out her spluttering.

"Anyway...escaped...Serpent's Chain...nonsense...," said the older woman.

Did she say *escaped?* Sophie strained to hear more. The toilet stopped flushing all of a sudden, and Sophie held her breath, her heart pounding in her chest so loudly she thought they would surely hear it.

The younger woman laughed, but her laugh seemed strained. "I don't know," she said, and her voice lowered. "There's a lot of cover-up going on, I think. What if the Serpent's Chain really has returned?"

"It's all ancient history—nothing to do with the Secretariat," said the older woman. "Heads roll, if there's some sort of cover-up going on though. Anyway, you'd hardly think the Serpent's Chain would pay any attention to MiddleGate, do you? It's probably got bigger snakes to snare elsewhere than in the Middle of Nowhere."

Serpent's Chain or not, thought Sophie, MiddleGate is not the Middle of Nowhere; and there are scads of snakes to snare.

iii The Oath

A stone dog grinned down at them.

FESTINA LENTE.
HURRY SLOWLY.

Mrs. Clop swept away a small cankerworm crawling across the counter. It flew through the air, landed on the floor near the column…and was still.

"I think that just about does it," said Mrs. Clop.

Wil wasn't sure whether *just about does it* referred to the cankerworm or him. But he was relieved to see the worm begin crawling slowly up the column toward the head of the stone dog.

"A couple more details. We should see the snake, of course, and the Oath—you have to take the Oath," said Mrs. Clop. "Mrs. Flyboottom, could you please get one of those gold seals."

Mrs. Flyboottom began to rummage in a drawer behind the counter and pulled out a gold seal, just as Sophie returned.

Wil noticed Sophie seemed agitated; her eyeglass frames were dark and shiny, like the black olives Aunt Violet loved. Wil had never seen Sophie's frames turn black—red and white polka dots, tiger strips, sunflower yellow, dull brown, yes…but never black.

Even her lenses seemed much darker than usual. Something's happened, he thought.

"Ah, the heroes!" said a familiar voice. Wil turned and found himself staring into the beaming face of Minister Skelch. His heart did a familiar flip-flop at the sight of the Minister, for Wil had been convinced for the longest time Minister Skelch, himself, was the mastermind behind the murder of the Narcisse snakes. It didn't matter Rufus Crookshank had turned out to be the real villain; Wil couldn't seem to shake his distrust of the Minister. There was something peculiar about the man, though Wil didn't know quite what.

"Hope you're being well taken care of, Mr. Wychwood. You and Miss Isidor have come to register your little snake, I take it?" said Minister Skelch. "Excellent. And are you going to introduce me to—?" He looked questioningly in Mr. Bertram's direction.

Wil was unable to do more than say, "Um—

"This is Mr. Bertram," said Sophie quickly. "He's the one who gave Esme to Wil."

"Ah, Mr. Bertram...Bertram, eh?" muttered Minister Skelch, reaching out to shake Mr. Bertram's hand. "Not Bartholomew Bertram, is it?" he asked.

To Wil's surprise, Mr. Bertram seemed shaken. "It's been a few years, hasn't it?" said Mr. Bertram.

"Yes, water under the bridge," said Minister Skelch heartily—a little too heartily, Wil thought, as though he were not saying what he was really thinking. "Miss Isidor, your Aunt Rue must be so proud of you. And Mr. Wychwood, I'm sure Mrs. Clop and Mrs. Flyboottom will take good care of you and that precious little snake of yours."

"Um...yes, sir," said Wil with a sidelong glance at Mrs. Clop, whose face had contorted itself into the semblance of a twisted smile.

"I've got his autograph right here, Minister," said Mrs. Flyboottom, brandishing the newspaper picture of Rufus Crookshank. "Imagine a known criminal living right here in MiddleGate under our very noses."

"Right," said Minister Skelch, his voice sharp.

"Would you like to meet Esme, Minister Skelch?" Wil asked.

"No, no, that's fine," said Minister Skelch. "Best be on my way," and he mumbled something about "lots of meetings, crises and other boring stuff," as he hurried off.

"All right, let's have a look," said Mrs. Clop. She stared into the cage without, it seemed, the slightest bit of curiosity, as if, she, Margaret Clop, had seen dozens of snakes before, and there could be nothing at all special about this particular representative of the species.

Mrs. Flyboottom, on the other hand, was clearly excited. "Yes, let's see this amazing little she-snake, shall we?" she exclaimed. "An historic moment!"

"You're not trying to fool us, are you?" asked Mrs. Clop, her voice flat and heavy, now that the Minister had left. "We're busy here, you know."

"What do you mean?" asked Wil.

"I mean, where is the snake?"

Wil looked into the cage and was horrified to see it was empty. He upended Esme's hut and scratched through the soil frantically.

Mr. Bertram shook his head. "She was in here when we left the house," he said. "I wonder if the cage door didn't snap shut when you slipped on the stairs, Wil."

A frenzied search of the counter revealed no Esme, until Mrs. Flyboottom pointed to the column and screeched, "Look, a snake, up there."

"Up there" high on the column was Esme. Coiled around the neck of the stone dog, she looked like a gleaming necklace worn by one of the ancient Egyptian pharaohs.

Wil ran to the bottom of the column. "Esme, please come back down," he whispered.

Esme's head wove from side to side; ever so slowly, she unwound herself…and dropped gracefully into Wil's outstretched hand. As Wil watched her slide into the pocket of his shirt, he saw the black medallion glinting through the fabric. With his back to the counter and sure that no one else could see what he was doing, he pulled out the gold chain with the black medallion and the gold ring. The sharp memory of his grandmother, Hazel Wychwood, flashed into his mind, for she had given him the medallion for his tenth birthday along with the large gold ring—just before her death.

Imagine, ten years old already! she had said, her voice shaking and her eyes tearing. You are a young man now. Never let these out of your sight. Always keep them with you.

The medallion's coin-sized disc hung from a crescent moon. On one side of the medallion, a silver triangle glimmered on the black matte surface. On the other side, the outline of a silver arrow with a tiny gold serpent at its tip glimmered. But today, to Wil's surprise, there was a new symbol on the medallion.

Wait until Sophie sees this, he thought. He quickly slipped the medallion under his shirt. Then he turned, pulled Esme from his pocket and put her back in the cage under the watchful eye of Mrs. Clop, who was tapping her fingers on the counter.

"Well, we've all seen the legendary snake," said Mrs. Clop. "Minister Skelch encouraged speedy processing of your Registration Application—but let me be clear we do not ever rubber-stamp Registration Applications in this office. Now, please repeat after me the Oath of Magykal Care. I, William Wychwood of MiddleGate—"

"I, William Wychwood of MiddleGate—" said Wil, his voice trembling.

"Do Hereby Solemnly—" Mrs. Clop coughed. "Do Hereby Solemnly Swear—" she repeated.

"Do Hereby...Solemnly Swear," said Wil.

"To Nurture, Feed and Shelter—" said Mrs. Clop, blurring all the words together.

"To Nurture...Feed and...and—" Wil's voice trailed off as he struggled to remember what else Mrs. Clop had said.

"And Shelter—" prompted Mrs. Flyboottom in a whisper.

"And Shelter—" said Wil, and he nodded gratefully to Mrs. Flyboottom.

Mrs. Clop frowned at Mrs. Flyboottom and said, "The Magykal Creature Known as Esme—"

"The Magykal Creature Known as Esme—" said Wil.

"Until Death Do Us Part." Mrs. Clop uttered these last words with an air of finality.

Wil gulped. "Until D-D-Death D-D-Do Us Part," he stuttered.

When all questions had finally been answered, and Wil had signed the Registration Application in triplicate, Mrs. Clop heaved a sigh of relief.

"Now there will be a slight charge, of course, to actually process this Registration Application," she said. "That will be ten doublers."

"Ten doublers?" asked Wil in dismay. It had never occurred to him registering Esme would cost money.

"Not to worry, my boy. There we go," said Mr. Bertram, as he handed Mrs. Clop a handful of the large silver coins known as doublers—they were engraved on one side with a two-headed snake.

"Thank you, Mr. Bertram," said Wil, wondering how Aunt Rue was going to pay Mr. Bertram back. She had seemed very worried about money recently and was snipping out more special offers and food coupons than ever from *The Daily Magezine.*

The licence was a small card and had Wil's name, Esme's name and a long number on it, all in fancy letters. Affixed in the bottom right corner was a shiny gold seal.

Owner: William Wychwood, MiddleGate
Magykal Creature: One egg-eating snake (Esme)
LICENCE NO. 026-1283191-7047603
Issued by the Secretariat on the Status
of Magical Creatures, MiddleGate
Per: Margaret Clop

"Why is the word magical spelled *m-a-g-y-k-a-l?* asked Wil.

Mrs. Clop frowned at the question, but Mrs. Flyboottom only laughed. "How observant you are, William Wychwood. *Magykal* with *yk* is the older spelling—more powerful too—still used in incantations and legal documents, dear. The Secretariat's name used to be spelled the old way too, but they decided to modernize it by dropping the *y* and *k* and using *i* and *c* instead."

With licence in hand at last, Wil felt vastly relieved. But his relief slid away when he glanced at Sophie's face. The frames of her eyeglasses were blacker than ever.

A smile lit up her face, however, when Mrs. Flyboottom said, "Sophie Isidor, don't you leave yet! My, how you've grown. Your Aunt Rue must be so proud. Could you autograph the newspaper too? There, beside William Wychwood. Imagine the two of you—standing right here at this counter!"

As they turned to leave, Wil heard Mrs. Flyboottom whisper to Mrs. Crop, "Did you hear the news on the radio early this morning? Didn't want to say anything while the children were here. The Snake in the Grass escaped in the middle of the night."

Escaped? thought Wil, hardly believing what he had just heard. Heese—I mean, Crookshank—escaped from the Firecatchers?

The frames of Sophie's glasses turned ashen white.

Mrs. Clop grimaced at Mrs. Flyboottom and jerked her head in Wil's and Sophie's direction.

As though suddenly aware Wil and Sophie—and Mr. Bertram—were still there, Mrs. Flyboottom smiled brightly at them and said in a business-like tone, "Anything more we can help you with?"

İV THE DEAD BEE

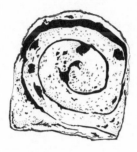

The world in a slice of bread.

O MUSA MYSTERIORUM,
NONNE QUAESTIONES EGENT RESPONSORUM?
AUDI PRECES NOSTRAS.
O MUSE OF MYSTERIES,
DO QUESTIONS NOT SEEK ANSWERS?
HEAR OUR PRAYERS.

It was already lunch time when Sophie, Wil and Esme finally returned home with Mr. Bertram. The house was filled with the mouth-watering smell of cinnamon raisin bread.

Wil set Esme's cage down in the living room, pulled out the licence from his pocket and waved it in the air. "Aunt Violet, we got it!" he said triumphantly.

"It certainly is an official-looking card with that gold seal, isn't it?" said Aunt Violet, peering at the licence. "And I thought you'd never return. I was beginning to get worried—especially after I read *Hedda's Horoscopes* in *The Daily Magezine.*"

"What does *Hedda's Horrorscopes* say, Aunt Violet?" asked Sophie, with a grin.

But Aunt Violet did not seem to think Sophie's joke was funny. She turned to the back page of *The Daily Magezine*. "Listen to this," she said, and her hair—which was already the colour of purple grape jelly—seemed to darken until it was almost black.

Celestial energies are unstable at present. This is an auspicious time for unveiling desires and ideals we struggle to hold tight, for they shield us from what we seek—the truth. Take advantage of this opportunity to weigh the consequences of your decisions. It is time to choose a course of action. But beware: the consequences of your decisions may be grave.

"And remember to eat your vegetables," said Sophie.

Aunt Violet glared at her. "One should not make fun of such things, Sophie."

"Doesn't it mean that whatever happens, whatever we decide to do, it's a serious thing?" asked Wil.

"Yes, and your decision may lead to the grave, my boy," quoted Aunt Violet ominously. "Whatever you decide today may have very dire consequences."

Wil and Sophie both shivered.

Mr. Bertram shook his head, obviously dismissing the daily horoscope. "Who knows what the future holds, Aunt Violet? Many soothsayers are the first to agree their advice is flimsy and open to conflicting interpretations—more for human amusement than any serious consideration."

"As you say, Bartholomew. But many of us—including you, no doubt—take comfort in having some guidance in their lives, however *flimsy!*" said Aunt Violet, her eyes flashing.

The sense of foreboding in the room only grew when Sophie and Wil told Aunt Violet Rufus Crookshank had escaped from the Firecatchers.

"There, I told you so. It is a dire day," said Aunt Violet, her face grim. "Children, why don't you carry your lunch into the garden— while it's still sunny," she said. "Bartholomew and I have some things to discuss."

❖❖❖❖❖❖

"Enough to give you the creeps," said Sophie, as she carried her lunch out to the bench in the garden. She took a big bite from her egg salad sandwich.

"Yeah. Aunt Violet sounded scary, didn't she?" said Wil and he looked over at the gargoyle, which, as usual, was glowering at him. It was an ill-tempered, ugly stone creature with a long spiral tail. Scarcely a cute garden ornament with its blunt snout, sharp teeth and bulbous eyes, and for some reason, it hated getting wet. It had been a favourite of Sophie's father, who had acquired it on one of his trips. Today, however, the usual tight, neat coil of its tail was slack.

Wil turned away from the gargoyle. "You don't think Aunt Violet's taking this reading-the-future too seriously—what did she call reading tea leaves the other day?

"Tasseomancy?" said Sophie.

"Right…tasseomancy. Do you know, last night, she took my tea cup and said, 'The tea leaves look like wings. Beware the wind, my boy, for it will carry you where you fear to go. Those wings are in the top sector of your cup, which means it may happen sooner rather than later.'"

Wil remembered reading the day's horoscope in the newspaper one morning when his grandmother had been alive. She had shaken her head impatiently. *Nothing but hocus-pocus bogus. Don't believe a sorcerer's word of it, William.*

"So what's the big *It* that's supposed to happen anyway?" asked Wil. "This tea leaf business seems fuzzy to me. I looked at those leaves in my cup; they were like two heads facing different directions."

"Portia and Portius?" suggested Sophie.

"Yeah, Portia and Portius," said Wil. "But so what? It doesn't tell you anything."

"Aunt Violet is probably just getting carried away," said Sophie. "She seems to be spending more and more time on tea leaves, doesn't she? And you're right, you can see anything you want to in them."

"Yeah," said Wil. He was about to take a bite from his sandwich when he stopped short.

"What's wrong?" asked Sophie, peering at the sandwich. "Is there a bug on it?"

"Can't you see it?" asked Wil.

"See what? It's a slice of bread with raisins—"

Sophie drew in a breath as Wil traced the spiral of brown sugar and cinnamon.

"A snake!" said Sophie. "Well, it doesn't matter. You can eat it anyway."

But Wil had lost his appetite.

"Anyway, wait until I tell you what happened in the bathroom," said Sophie. "There was a sign on the door of the bathroom stall— only I didn't see it at first—*Do Not Use. Out of Order.*"

"So?" said Wil.

"Well, I was in that stall, and two women were talking, but they didn't know I was there. And they were talking about magical bees and honey and something else—an *apiponis destructor.*

"What's an *apiponis destructor?*" asked Wil. "I don't like the *destructor* part."

"Whatever it is, one of the women—I think it was the younger one—I think she said it was a matter of national security."

"National security? That's huge, isn't it?"

"Yeah. But it was hard to hear any more, because the toilet kept on flushing and flushing—but I think she said the Serpent's Chain was involved somehow."

"So that's why you were gone so long," said Wil. "I thought we'd never finish registering Esme. That Mrs. Clop asked me for the birth date, and I thought she meant Esme's birthday, but she really meant *my* birth date. I don't think she wanted to give me a licence."

"When's your birthday?" interrupted Sophie, her mouth full of sandwich.

"August 21st."

"But that's my birthday too! We have the exact same birthday," squealed Sophie, the frames of her glasses turning pink.

"The exact same birthday," repeated Wil, looking down again at the spiral snake on his bread. "Really weird," he said slowly." Want to hear something else that's really weird? Esme escaped from her cage and climbed up that column at the Secretariat. When I managed to get her back down, I could see the medallion shining through my shirt. And when I held it in my hand, beside the serpent, there was another gold symbol."

"What was it?" asked Sophie, her eyes wide.

"You won't believe me," said Wil.

"Well?"

"It was a golden bee." As soon as he said the words, Wil felt a tingling at the back of his neck and the medallion suddenly felt warm.

"A bee!" said Sophie, her frames turning lollipop yellow.

"Ssssh...or you'll have Aunt Violet out here," said Wil, whispering, "and she'll be telling us both we're going to *depart this earthly plain.*"

"Remember the list of things in *The Daily Magezine?*" asked Sophie. "All those things they found in Crookshank's pocket?"

Wil nodded.

"There was a dead bee—and an empty vial," said Sophie. She grinned and her glass frames shouted a dazzling yellow—the kind of yellow Wil would choose to be if he had to be yellow, he thought. "Maybe we have to crack another mystery!" she said mischievously.

Wil heard Miss Heese's—no, it was Rufus Crookshank's—voice hissing like a steaming kettle. *Yesss, the tasksss, you must do the black medallion's tasks-s-s-s.*

"Crookshank told me I'd have to do the black medallion's tasks," said Wil, pulling out the medallion, "or it—the medallion—would... would kill me."

Sophie looked down at the medallion. "Well, there's no bee now," she said in a matter-of-fact way. "And how could a tiny piece of jewellery kill you? Are you sure you didn't imagine that bee?"

"Of course not," said Wil, his cheeks flushing. "Maybe you only imagined what you heard in the bathroom with the running toilet."

"Okay, sorry," said Sophie, stroking the medallion with her finger. "First the snakes of Narcisse, and now we've got to help these magical bees, or whatever they are."

V A BumBLEBEE

The bumblebee had had enough of human noise.

QUICUMQUE APE PUNCTUS EST
UMBRAM EIUS TIMET.
ONCE STUNG BY A BEE,
NOW AFRAID OF A BEE'S SHADOW

As Sophie and Wil walked back to Gruffud's Academy after lunch, the sky began to cloud over. A cool wind from the north was blowing through the elm trees and cankerworm webs kept getting tangled in their hair, as if clouding their thoughts.

They circled around the Brimstone Snakes monument in Grunion Square. The monument was now cordoned off, with two guards standing nearby. Sophie shuddered at the memory of the man in the black cloak and hood—he had turned out to be Rufus Crookshank—sitting on top of the monument. The man had muttered, *"Umbra nullam umbram facit."* A shadow casts no shadow. Then he had pulled Sophie through the Brimstone Snakes into a roaring whirl of frozen air—a magical portal to Narcisse. But with Esme's help, Wil's shadow had swallowed up Crookshank's shadow that day, as if Wil were a master snapdragon champion.

There was one thing she had never managed to figure out, however.

"How *did* Mr. Bertram find us at Narcisse anyway?" asked Sophie.

"I don't know," said Wil as he scuffled a stone down the sidewalk. "He just appeared. He must have seen the note about the Brimstone Snakes I left on the kitchen table. I was trying to hold down Crookshank's shadow. There was this stabbing cold, and the next moment I heard a hissing sound, like thousands of snakes singing; it felt like a warm breeze. And Mr. Bertram was standing there. I thought you found him when you ran to get help."

"But I twisted my ankle and could hardly walk, remember?" said Sophie.

"He must have heard you calling for help," said Wil.

"I don't think so," said Sophie. "But I drew a picture on the ground."

"Of what?" asked Wil.

"A large bird with wide wings," said Sophie. "I remember saying, *I wish I had wings like you.* The sky went a little dark, as if the sun was being covered by a cloud for a moment."

"Well, maybe your drawing was like a secret message," said Wil, "Or maybe snapdragon shadows send out powerful signals, or something. Or maybe Mr. Bertram somehow heard the snakes of Narcisse hissing. Anyway, it doesn't really matter now, does it?"

"No," said Sophie, "I guess not. We *did* capture Rufus Crookshank."

"Even if he did escape," said Wil, shaking his head ruefully.

"Do you know we only have thirteen more days of school until the holidays?" asked Sophie abruptly.

"No more putting up with insults from Sygnithia and Sylvain. Yes!" said Wil, punching the air. "But I wish the library was open. I wonder who's going to be the librarian now."

"What about Mr. Bertram?" said Sophie. "Maybe he could come and live in MiddleGate."

"I bet he'd make a really great librarian," said Wil slowly. "That would be amazing, wouldn't it? He can find any book."

❖❖❖❖❖❖

Cartology class had not yet begun when Sophie and Wil arrived. Mage Tibor's classroom walls were plastered with maps from all over the world, and star plots wrapped the ceiling. Even the floor was painted with great concentric circles charting the movements of the planets across the skies. Today, Mage Tibor's desk was covered in a dark cloth. Wil wondered what was underneath it.

Mage Tibor's face broke into a wide smile as they entered. He adjusted his blue half-spectacles and clapped his hands.

"Class, as a bit of a surprise, I think a little...hmmm...celebration is in order, don't you?

"To think a portal from MiddleGate to Narcisse was...hmmm... here all this time! There are many—naysayers, those—who thought my curious...hmmm...quest for another portal in MiddleGate was doomed to failure."

He spoke in a high, squeaky voice, as if imitating one of those naysayers. "Secret gates and doors—can the poor man think of nothing else?"

Everyone in the class laughed.

Even if Mage Tibor were a little odd—with those dark blue half-spectacles on his nose, it was a wonder he could read anything at all, and his hmmm's were really annoying, thought Wil. But the man had such a love of maps, it was hard not to be excited by his contagious enthusiasm. And it wasn't as if all the teachers at Gruffud's weren't a little strange, each in their own way. His favourite teacher, Mage Terpsy—the verbology teacher—was always mixing up her sentences. One of her better slips—*the poxes are biled one on top of the other* instead of *the boxes are piled.* And Mage Adderson, the numeristics teacher, was one of the most sour people Wil had ever met; usually she had nothing but sharp words for her students.

"Now, have I not been proven right?" said Mage Tibor. Wil had the feeling Mage Tibor would have liked nothing better than to parade in front of all those who had insulted his work, chanting *I told you so.*

"Our search has been vindicated, and just before the end of this school term too. All because of Sophie Isidor and William Wychwood! Who can tell us what lessons this tale holds?" asked Mage Tibor gleefully.

Harley Weeks's hand shot into the air. As always, Harley seemed to have a permanent smile pasted onto his face.

"Yes, Mr. Weeks? What did you learn from this story?"

"Never, ever give up," said Harley, pretending to have a deep voice.

"Good start," said Mage Terpsy. "What else?"

Wil's only thought was that without a friend like Esme, the story could have had a very different ending; but he didn't want to say so. He was sure Sylvain Sly and his sister Sygnithia (as much a tormentor as her brother) would make fun of him.

Mage Tibor took a deep breath and launched into a speech.

"Well...hmmm...have we not taken the Brimstone Snakes for granted? Have those two snakes not coiled faithfully through rain and sleet and snow? Did we not all climb to the top of the snakes' heads when we were young children and pretend to fly to the stars?

"But who could know...with the right incantation...hmmm...and the rainbow's arc, the Brimstone Snakes would become a magical gateway, a portal beyond MiddleGate?

"Inspect closely what seems most *ordinary;* it may, in fact, be most extraordinary. Thank you, Miss Isidor and Mr. Wychwood!"

Everyone in the class clapped—except for Sygnithia and Sylvain. They only frowned—neither of them had a good word to say about Sophie's family, ever since Sophie's father, Cyril Isidor, had been suspected of murdering the MiddleGate librarian ten years ago and then disappeared.

From what Wil had managed to piece together, Cyril Isidor's family and friends—including Mr. Bertram—had all come under the shadow of suspicion. Sophie's mother had turned strange after his disappearance and been accused of covering up for her husband; she too vanished a short time thereafter. Thus it was the two cousins, both of them orphaned, had come to live with Aunt Rue and Aunt Violet—for Wil had also lost both his parents when he was a baby and his grandmother was killed in a mysterious fire the previous summer. Cyril Isidor's study door was now kept locked; only Aunt Rue entered to water the plants. She never seemed never to give up hope her brother might return some day and lit a candle for him in the kitchen windowsill each night.

Ten years was a long time, thought Wil.

✦✦✦✦✦✦

"Yes, a true lesson for us all," said Mage Tibor. "As one of my favourite poets, Esther Bragwell, proclaimed…hmmm—" He began to recite a verse from some poem, which must have been written by Esther Bragwell herself.

*Lady Luck moves not
Heaven and Earth.
By every flower and herb,
By cactus, by weed
They shall inspire,
These bustling bees
No haste, no greed
No harm, no ire—*

Sophie could hear someone whispering behind her and turned her head to listen.

"Why's he going on about bees?" Harley Weeks was whispering to Olin Cramer.

"My grandfather said that if someone gets stung by a bee, they'll probably be afraid of a bee's shadow forever and ever," Olin whispered back. "Did you know there was a boy in France who got stung by more than a thousand bees when he was bicycling by a sunflower field?"

"Did he…did he die?" asked Harley, clearly horrified.

From the corner of her eye, Sophie saw Olin nod his head grimly.

Sophie had never thought about a bee having a shadow. She supposed it would be a small shadow. And the thought of more than a thousand bee stings was beyond imagining. Sometimes Olin was prone to exaggerating, but for some reason, his story rang true. And if it really was true— well…Sophie could not bear to think about that boy in France.

"—everyone's eyes are on my desk," said Mage Tibor. "You are wondering…hmmm…what is underneath that cloth? In honour of the occasion, shall we—" He whipped the cover from his desk and the class broke into cheers.

"Shall we have some…hmmm…snakecake?" said Mage Tibor.

There, sitting in all its glory, was a humongous snakecake—a striped black-and-white layer cake, frosted in shimmering, silver, candied scales—the largest Sophie had ever seen. It was almost as big as the MiddleGate Bus's steering wheel. She glanced over at Wil, for snakecake was his all-time favourite treat.

Wil grinned back at her.

But before anyone could enjoy one bite of the rich cake, Regina Piehard pointed at the snakecake. "A bee! There's a bee," she squealed.

And sure enough, a bumblebee was squatting like a tiny gold lion right in the middle of the snakecake. The furry little animal stared impudently out at the whole class and buzzed its wings.

"Only a little...rather, a big...bee," said Mage Tibor, pushing his glasses further down on his nose to inspect the bumblebee. "My wee warrior princess! And I was just reciting that old Bragwell poem about bees, wasn't I?" He chuckled. "One of those convergences when the earth's energies meet."

"Mage Tibor, that's the biggest bumblebee I've ever seen," said Olin.

"I think, Mr. Cramer, you may be right.

"Mr. Wychwood, since you're closest to the window, would you be so kind as to...hmmm...open it?" said Mage Tibor.

Wil jumped up to open the window, but apparently unaware Sygnithia Sly had stuck out her foot, he tripped against Mage Tibor's desk. His left hand smashed into the snakecake and narrowly missed squashing the bumblebee.

"What in snake's name!" exclaimed Mage Tibor.

The bumblebee zoomed high into a corner of the window, where it buzzed recklessly against the window.

Sophie could almost hear its *Let me out, let me out!*

"Nice going, Wormwood," jeered Sygnithia, as Wil stumbled back to his stool, his hand smeared with snakecake icing and candied scales.

Sophie glared at Sygnithia, who only shrugged and rolled her eyes.

The bumblebee zipped up to the ceiling, hovered by the star plot of the Southern hemisphere, plunged to the floor—so startling Mage Tibor that his blue half-spectacles fell to the floor.

The bumblebee made a last swoop and landed noisily on the

bright yellow ribbon on Regina's unsuspecting head.

The bumblebee must think the ribbon is a sunflower, thought Sophie.

"Help—it's going to sting me!" screeched Regina, who began to dance around the room, her arms flailing in the air. She reminded Sophie of a marionette with snarled strings.

Everyone in the class began to laugh.

Whipping from side to side, the bumblebee clutched the yellow ribbon.

"Please do not move, Miss Piehard," bellowed Mage Tibor. "Leave a bee alone and the bee will leave you alone.

"Honeybees die if they sting someone—the barbed stinger gets stuck in the victim and rips out from the bee's body. But bumblebees have smooth stingers. They can sting multiple times. But I assure you, Miss Piehard, this humble bumblebee does not want to sting you."

But at Mage Tibor's words *stuck, victim* and *rips,* Regina only screeched all the more.

Suddenly, as if it had had enough of human hullabaloo, the bumblebee spiralled upward, skimmed past Mage Tibor's head, circled slowly around the snakecake (and regretfully, Sophie imagined), and then looped out the window, over the grass and past the large boulder in front of Gruffud's Academy. It was quickly lost to view.

Mage Tibor handed a cloth to Wil and smiled broadly. "Snakecake, anyone? Hmmm…can't let all this go to waste!" he exclaimed, as he cut a generous slice of snakecake and held it high in the air. "Any takers? Miss Piehard?

"Drone bees—the male bees—don't have stingers at all of course, and the stingers on all queen bees are smooth, for those of you who are interested."

❖❖❖❖❖

Regina Piehard refused to eat any of the cake.

And Sophie hardly tasted her slice. She had been spellbound by the bumblebee's steep, buzzing nose-dive—right underneath Mage Tibor's nose.

I wonder what it would be like to be a bee, she thought.

Vİ A Pall of Darkness

Its contents were as black as the shadows.

VOCO VINCO VOLO.
I CHALLENGE, I CONQUER, I SOAR.

Two shadowy figures glided from the dark glade of trees near the Gruffud's Academy greenhouse. In the stillness of that summer night, the waning moon, a dark orb but for the faintest silver sliver, cast its pale light on the seven beehives. It was a stillness soaked in the smell of lilac blossoms. A stillness broken only by the soft humming of the bees.

"Are you sure this is safe?" whispered a woman's voice.

"This is no time for fear," answered a man's voice. "Few understand the true powers-s-s of the ambrosia. But in the hands of the Serpent's Chain—"

"Sssshhh," said the woman. "Did you hear that? Something flew overhead."

"Only a bat," said the man.

"Be quick," hissed the woman. "We should have invoked the invisibility enchantment."

"That would do us no good here," replied the man. "You worry too much. The *artes magicae* will do their work."

The man pulled a star-shaped glass vial from his pocket and held it up in the dim moonlight. Its contents were as black as the shadows. He pulled out the stopper and tipped the vial over each of the beehives. Black clouds swirled over the hives. The pall of darkness blanketed the beehives and slowly dissolved.

The humming of the bees lulled.

Silence.

"Voco vinco volo," whispered the man and woman together.

VĬĬ Black Honey

True honey connoisseurs sniff honey
to appreciate its perfume before they taste it.

UBI MEL, IBI APES.
WHERE THERE ARE BEES, THERE IS HONEY.

It was a stifling hot, airless day at the end of the first week in July. Mr. Bertram had returned several days ago to Toronto, and Aunt Rue had left for work at the S.S.M.C. early that morning and was not due back until after supper time.

With school out for the summer, Wil and Sophie were lolling about in the living room, with nothing much to do. All Wil's ideas had shrivelled up like stale, dried raisins. He was working on T*he Daily Magezine* crossword puzzle but it was not going well. He had only solved three words so far.

Sophie's glass frames were brown, the colour of bruised peaches. She was half-heartedly drawing a portrait of her cat Cadmus, who was splayed out on the living room floor, looking mostly dead, but for the occasional twitch of his striped tail.

And Aunt Violet was sitting at the kitchen table peering into her tea cup and muttering to herself. The last few days, she had been plying Wil and Sophie with copious cups of peppermint tea, and Wil was getting tired of picking out the leaves from his teeth. As soon as they finished their cups—and sometimes even before they had finished—Aunt Violet whisked the tea cups from them and fervently inspected the dregs.

When Wil had asked her what she was doing, she only gave him a peculiar look—half secretive, half conspiratorial—and said, "I'm practicing."

"Practicing what?" Wil had asked.

"Reading the leaves, of course!"

"But why?"

"I'm just practicing!" she had said indignantly.

Sophie erased Cadmus's tail for the seventh time from her drawing and sighed. "Cadmus keeps moving his tail," she said. "You want to do something, Wil?"

"Sure," replied Wil, throwing the puzzle aside. "You got any ideas?" he asked hopefully.

"Does Esme need any quail eggs?" she asked. "Maybe we could go to the egg shop."

"Nope, we've still got some," said Wil. "And Esme's not been eating much lately anyway."

"Children, why don't you go and get some honey," said Aunt Violet. "We're almost out, and I want to make some pastries for the Herb Society meeting. Get a nice light New Zealand honey if Melilla Morggan has any. And could you also please ask her for a cake of beeswax."

"What are you going to do with the beeswax, Aunt Violet?" asked Sophie.

"My grandmother used to pour melted beeswax into cold water," said Aunt Violet. "She told fortunes from the shapes formed, as the beeswax cooled. I thought I'd like to try it out."

"Does that mean we won't have to drink so much tea?" said Sophie immediately.

Aunt Violet only laughed.

❖❖❖❖❖

Sophie and Wil walked along Half Moon Lane past Earbend Street, Wog's Hollow and Rolling Fork Street towards Stricker Street. The houses were all tilted at odd angles, some of them so crooked, they seemed to be gradually sinking into the earth. The roads themselves were mostly quiet; MiddleGate seemed to have emptied for the holidays.

Melilla's Honey Shop on Stricker Street featured a large storefront window and shelves chock-full with gleaming jars of honey. Powdered honey, blueberry honey, honeyed almonds, honey infused with cinnamon, honeyed chocolate, and honeycomb. Jars with honeys as clear as water, honeys with a pickle green tinge, golden and amber honeys, creamed honeys, and one so dark, it looked like black bootstrap molasses. The jars had beautiful labels with pictures of flowers and bees from all over the world.

And there was the shelf of honeys from New Zealand. Unfamiliar, musical names that Sophie and Wil tried to pronounce...*tawari, kamahi, manuka, pohutukawa.*

"Sounds like a secret incantation," Wil said, as he scribbled the names down in his notebook.

The woman who ran the shop, Melilla Morggan, was standing behind the counter and talking to a tall woman with pale, parchment-like skin and shiny hair as black as a crow's tail. On the counter between them sat several small jars of honey.

Sophie overhead the woman with the black hair say in a hoarse voice, "The Secretariat is quite concerned about the security of honey supplies. But your prices are too high."

"There are others who will pay for this liquid gold," replied Melilla Morggan stiffly.

As Wil and Sophie approached the counter, the black-haired woman turned her head to look at them. It was chilling how swiftly her face changed its expression, as soon as she caught sight of Wil. Her look of anger was swiftly replaced by one of shock. Her parchment face tightened, and her eyes became blank, expressionless. It was as if a cloak had suddenly been thrown over her eyes, thought Sophie.

The black-haired woman moved to the other side of the shop and began to look at other jars of honey, but Sophie had the feeling she wasn't really seeing them.

Melilla Morggan glanced apprehensively at the black-haired woman and then smiled at Sophie and Wil.

"What can I do for you today, children?" she asked brightly.

"Aunt Violet would like some honey from New Zealand, Mrs. Morggan," said Sophie.

"Well, you're in luck," said Melilla Morggan, "as we received a new shipment this morning." She pulled out a bottle of honey from a crate and placed it on the counter. "I'm sure Aunt Violet will love this new vipers bugloss honey," she said.

"That sounds like a snake, not honey," Wil whispered to Sophie.

Melilla Morggan laughed. "A vintage honey from New Zealand's south island, my dears. Definitely not a snake! Lovely, light floral nectar from the delicate vipers bugloss plant *(echium vulgare)*—also known as blueweed, blue thistle and even blue devil in some parts. The clean taste of blue summer sky, if ever there was one, and a good tonic against fatigue—helps to strengthen the heart too. Can I get anything else for you?"

Sophie shook her head.

"Didn't Aunt Violet want some beeswax too?" asked Wil.

"Oh, right," said Sophie.

"One package of beeswax coming right up," said Melilla Morggan. "And why don't you try a sample of *Today's Special*—my favourite, our local buckwheat honey." She held out an open jar of the black honey, which Sophie looked at dubiously.

"One of the richest, most nutritious honeys," said Melilla Morggan appreciatively.

The black honey looked like some disagreeable combination of tar, oil, wet dirt, dark sugar and molasses, thought Sophie...with something slushy in the middle.

"The honey has just crystallized a little," said Melilla Morggan encouragingly.

Revolting, thought Sophie. Although she didn't know it, the frames of her glasses had suddenly turned the colour of the black honey.

"True honey connoisseurs," said Melilla Morggan, "sniff honey to appreciate its perfume before they taste it." She took two small wooden spoons, dipped them in the jar of black honey and held them out with a big smile. "Some do say it's an acquired taste."

Sophie took the small wooden spoon and sniffed the honey. It smelled like perfume no one would ever buy.

From Wil's expression, he must have felt the same way.

Under Melilla Morggan's watchful gaze—it was impossible to refuse her offer without seeming rude—Wil and Sophie licked their spoons.

Sophie reeled from the buckwheat honey's dark sweetness; an overwhelming smell of barnyard filled her mouth.

"Thank you, Mrs. Morggan," said Sophie weakly, wishing she could have several glasses of water to wash out her mouth.

Wil smiled bravely and nodded. "It's really…really good," he said, but his voice didn't sound very convincing, thought Sophie.

Thanking Melilla Morggan, they quickly paid for the vipers bugloss honey and beeswax, then scurried past the black-haired woman. They were about to leave the shop when Sophie noticed a small notice on the bulletin board beside the shop door.

"Wil, look," she said excitedly.

HELP WANTED
Beekeeping
Contact Mage Radix, Gruffud's Academy

"So?" said Wil, after he scanned the notice. "You're kidding, right?"

"Come on. It'll be fun. Besides, what else have we got to do?"

Wil only grunted and stepped out on the street. When they had turned the corner onto Half Moon Lane, he asked, "You know that black-haired woman?"

"She looked at you really strangely," said Sophie.

"It was a little creepy," said Wil. "Who was she?"

"I don't know," said Sophie. "But her voice reminded me of that older woman in the washroom at the Secretariat. I didn't manage to get a good look at her then—except through the crack in the door."

"Did you see how her eyes went blank when she saw me?" asked Wil.

"She must have been hiding something," said Sophie. "And did you see that honey on the counter—the honey they were arguing about?"

"No," said Wil. "You know, I'm still trying to forget the taste of that black honey. Worst honey I've ever tasted. It shouldn't even be called honey!"

"Don't you notice anything?" said Sophie.

"Okay, what was wrong with the honey on the counter?" said Wil.

"It had red streaks in it," said Sophie.

"You mean like streaks of blood?" asked Wil.

"Yeah, it did remind me of blood," said Sophie. "And Mrs. Morggan locked the jars in a drawer. I wonder what kind of honey it was."

"Nothing I'd want to taste," said Wil.

As they approached home, Wil pointed to the end of the street. "Look at that!" he exclaimed.

The grass in front of the house at the end of the street was as green as a frog—quite at odds with all the other lawns, which were turning yellow, for it hadn't rained in some days.

And the crooked FOR SALE sign, which had hung in front for so many years, was freshly painted and straight.

Sophie couldn't believe her eyes. "They're trying to sell the house for real," she said.

Viii Tea Bag and Bee-Tag

Only when Sophie mentioned the words bees and honey,
did Aunt Rue's eyes focus on her.

APIARIUS DIXIT TEMPUS ADVENIRE
MEDITARI MULTAS RES :
ANISOPTERAS, ALAS MELLITAS
ET QUOD SI APES CANTENT.
THE TIME HAS COME THE BEEKEEPER SAID
TO MUSE ON MANY THINGS
OF DRAGONFLIES AND HONEYED WINGS
OF HOW THE BEE DOTH SING.

Aunt Violet, her purple flowered dress dusted with flour, was bustling about the kitchen. Frazzled strands of purple hair were flying in all directions and her purple glasses were askew. A mound of luscious crullers drizzled with vipers bugloss honey was growing in anticipation of the next Herb Society meeting. "If you're both good, as a special treat, you can share one cruller tonight," she told Sophie and Wil.

Supper that night was but a simple affair with boiled potatoes and spinach salad. Wil sighed at the sight of the spinach—not his favourite vegetable. Lately, dinners seemed to have been slipping, thought

Wil, gazing longingly at the crullers. Perhaps the summer's humidity was too much for Aunt Violet. She didn't do well in the heat and kept mopping her brow every few minutes.

Or perhaps it had something to do with the fact Aunt Rue was hardly ever home for dinner any more—and even when she was, she didn't seem to notice what she was eating, despite Aunt Violet's entreaties. Aunt Rue was being given more and more responsibility at work—although Wil wasn't sure exactly what that meant. He had overheard her complaining to Aunt Violet one night that her salary was barely enough to support the household and with all her new responsibilities, surely they should be giving her a raise as well.

Tonight, Aunt Rue had deep circles under her eyes and her two coiled, grey braids were thinner than ever. She hardly seemed to listen when Sophie and Wil bubbled on excitedly about the green grass at the end of Half Moon Lane.

"You know, the house at the end of the street, the one with the crooked FOR SALE sign, only it's not crooked now?" said Sophie. "The grass was so green it looked fake, like it had been painted."

"Perhaps we'll finally have some new neighbours," said Aunt Violet after a quick glance at the silent Aunt Rue, who was toying with her boiled potato.

Only when Sophie mentioned the words bees and honey did Aunt Rue's eyes focus on her.

"I'm sorry, dear. What did you say?"

"There was a notice on the board at Melilla's, Aunt Rue. Mage Radix needs some help with beekeeping," repeated Sophie. "Can we do it? Please? Then we won't be bored."

"Both of you?" asked Aunt Rue and she looked over at Wil.

Wil gulped—he wasn't sure he wanted to help Mage Radix with the bees. Olin Cramer's story about the boy in France who had been stung to death was a little scary.

But when Sophie kicked his leg under the table, he mustered a grin. "Yeah, me too," he said.

Aunt Rue exchanged looks with Aunt Violet, as if to say, *Do you think this is a good idea?*

Aunt Violet nodded her head imperceptibly.

"Well, I'm not sure," said Aunt Rue. "You could invite some friends over to play, you know."

"Everyone's away for the summer," said Sophie, nibbling at one of her fingernails.

"Yeah," said Wil, knowing full well this was a complete lie. But they couldn't very well admit to Aunt Rue and Aunt Violet they didn't have any friends. Aunt Rue and Aunt Violet couldn't possibly understand. Even if he and Sophie had invited someone over, they probably wouldn't have come, or their parents would have found some excuse. He'd seen the look of pity or downright scorn in people's faces and heard the whispering that stopped suddenly when he and Sophie walked by. Even though he and Sophie had helped save the snakes of Narcisse, there was still a cloud of suspicion hanging over the Isidor family—a cloud as dark as it had been ten years ago when Sophie's father, Cyril Isidor, had been suspected of murdering the MiddleGate Librarian.

"Why can't we help Mage Radix?" asked Sophie.

"Please don't bite your fingernails, Sophie," said Aunt Rue. "I'm not at liberty to say much, but you'll remember I was working on a bee fungus report. The Department of Endangered Insects at the Secretariat has been concerned that some of the honeybees are falling sick."

"Why are they getting sick?" asked Wil. "Is it something to do with an *apiponis destructor?*"

Aunt Rue's forehead wrinkled. "What do you know about the *apiponis destructor?*" she said, her voice sounding strained.

"We heard someone...someone else talking about it," said Sophie quickly, with a warning glare at Wil. "We don't even know what an *apiponis* is."

"The *apiponis destructor* is a kind of mite, a small parasite that lives on bees," said Aunt Rue. "But it could be other things," she said darkly.

"What other things?" asked Sophie, as she carried dishes to the sink.

Aunt Rue began to stack the dishes noisily, and Aunt Violet said briskly, "Time to get ready for bed, children."

Aunt Rue knew much, much more than she was telling, thought Sophie

"At any rate, I'll speak to Mage Radix tomorrow," said Aunt Rue, "and see what can be arranged."

Wil pulled out an old tea bag from the tea pot and was about to put it in the compost when he suddenly thought of Mage Terpsy.

"Tea bag," he said as he held up the limp, dripping bag.

"For snake's sake, Wil, what are you doing?" said Aunt Violet. "You're dripping all over the clean floor."

"Tea bag," repeated Wil and he danced around the kitchen, waving the tea bag. "Can't you see? A *tipsy-terpsy*!"

Sophie's eyes lit up. "Bee-tag!" she said, wondering whether the golden bee had appeared again on Wil's medallion.

"What are you two talking about?" scolded Aunt Violet, and she grabbed the tea bag from Wil. "To bed with the both of you, this instant. No cruller for you tonight."

✦✦✦✦✦

Esme glided gracefully from Wil's arms back into her cage beside his bed. Wil yawned and turned the light out, but instead of darkness, his room filled with a glowing light.

The light was coming from the medallion around his neck. The figure of the golden bee was shining brightly again beside the medallion's serpent. His heart racing, Wil snuck out of his bedroom and down the hall to Sophie's room. Her light was still on. He knocked quietly.

"Wil, is that you?" Sophie answered. "Don't come in yet."

Wil heard what sounded like a drawer being slammed shut.

"Okay, you can come in now," said Sophie.

Wil opened the door. The strong smell of paint, or something like it, assailed his nostrils.

Sophie's room was papered with more drawings than ever of fantastical creatures—drawings on the wall, the ceiling, the mirror, her bed...everywhere. Even Cadmus, who was sleeping on the bed, was half-hidden by a drawing of a dragonfly with ginormous wings.

Sophie was sitting on the bed amidst all the papers. She looked embarrassed and was sitting on her hands, but Wil hardly noticed.

"Remember I told you about the bee on the medallion and how it was glowing the day we went to the Secretariat to register Esme?" he said all in one breath.

Sophie only stared at him wide-eyed.

"Well, turn off your light," Wil demanded.

"Why?"

"Just turn it off," said Wil.

The light from the medallion glowed in the darkened room, then began to fade slowly until the room was completely dark.

"You were right," whispered Sophie.

"Of course I was right," said Wil impatiently. "Did you think I made it up?"

"We really do have another task, just like I said," whispered Sophie. She turned the light on and both of them blinked in the glare. "It's like the medallion is telling us what to do," said Sophie.

"You don't think it has a mind of its own, do you?" said Wil, looking down at the medallion.

"What did your grandmother tell you about the medallion and the gold ring?" asked Sophie.

"Not much. They belonged to my parents and I'm not supposed to let the medallion and the gold ring out of my sight."

Sophie brightened. "I bet if we're going to find out what's wrong with the bees, we'll have to turn into bees ourselves."

"Turn into bees?" said Wil. "I don't want to turn into a bee—what a bad idea."

He could hear in his mind what his grandmother would have had to say about all this. *William, what can you be thinking of? Is this how I raised you? You can't be serious. There's no such thing as magic.*

"Who wants to go inside a beehive?" he continued. "Didn't you hear Olin telling that story about the boy who got stung by more than a thousand bees?"

Sophie was silent. Then she said, "You're right. It's just that Aunt Rue seems so worried all the time. You don't think she'd lose her job, do you? They obviously don't know what's going on at the Secretariat.

No one knows whether there's some weird fungus or bee mites, or whatever they're called."

"And that woman at Melilla's Honey Shop said something about the security of honey supplies," said Wil. "Maybe they're starting to run out of honey because of whatever's hurting the bees."

"Well, if we could save the snakes of Narcisse, we'll figure out a way to help the magical bees," said Sophie.

Sophie's voice sounded far more confident than Wil felt, especially when he heard Aunt Violet's heavy footsteps came up the stairs.

"Quick," whispered Wil. "Turn off the light!"

"You can't fool me," said Aunt Violet, breathing heavily and sounding cross. She stood shadowed in the doorway. "Children, it's almost midnight. What in serpent's name are you still doing awake? Enough scheming, the both of you!"

"Good night, Aunt Violet," said Wil, as he scuttled past her. He was surprised to see she was carrying a stack of books and a copy of the *Burning Heart* magazine with the cover of the crystal ball.

ıx ȷ vпк

Why would anyone throw this out?

NUM QUISQUILIAE? IMMO, THESAURI!
JUNK? NO, 'TIS TREASURE!

Although it was still early in the morning, the summer heat was festering. Aunt Violet and Aunt Rue were out doing the week's food shopping, leaving Sophie and Wil with strict instructions not to leave the house.

"Children, we'll be gone only a short time and we'll need your help with the groceries when we return," said Aunt Rue.

As soon as they left, Sophie clapped her hands. The frames of her eyeglasses changed from mud-brown to green.

"Let me guess," said Wil. "You're going to say, *Let's go see the house that's for sale.*"

"How did you know?" asked Sophie, with a look of surprise.

Wil merely shrugged. "Lucky guess," he said.

"Shall we go?" said Sophie.

"But we're supposed to stay in the house," said Wil, sneaking a glance at Aunt Violet's crullers. He had been hoping they would get to have one at lunch. But if Aunt Violet found out they'd left the house...

"They'll be gone for an hour or more, and anyway, we're only going down to the end of the street," said Sophie. "We'll leave a note on the table, in case they come back early."

The heat hit their faces as they stepped outside, but at least there was a wind today. Small grey clouds were whisking across the sky.

The lawn was more brilliant than ever—as green as the spinach they'd had for supper last night. The sidewalk in front of the house had been swept and the windows were sparkling. There were even white flowers, their edges stained pink, waving in a large pot on the porch. The FOR SALE sign was swaying hypnotically. But the house still had a dismal air about it, thought Wil. It looked unloved. The peeling paint and overgrown bushes only added to the general air of neglect.

"It still looks like no one has lived here for years," said Wil.

"Well, they haven't," said Sophie.

They crept up the front stairs and peered in one of the windows. Inside was gloomy and dark. White sheets covered stuffed chairs and sofas, and cobwebs hung from a large chandelier.

"Do you know who used to live here?" asked Wil.

"No," said Sophie. "All I know is the FOR SALE sign has been hanging out front since forever," said Sophie. "It's strange, but I thought I saw a light flickering in one of the windows last night."

Wil felt the hairs on the back of his neck stand up. "Maybe there's a ghost," he said, thinking of Peeping Peerslie, the ghost who lived in the MiddleGate Library. Peeping Peerslie was an invisible ghost, for no one had ever seen him—aptly named, because he looked over people's shoulders and tried to help them with their homework, whether they wanted help or not. He wondered what Peeping Peerslie was doing now that the MiddleGate Library was closed.

"Anyway, it was probably the real estate agent and someone came to inspect the house last night," said Sophie. "Let's go around the back."

As they turned the corner of the house, they heard voices.

"Someone's coming," whispered Wil. "Come on. Quick! We'll have to hide in the bushes."

They ducked under a juniper bush in the nick of time, as two people came up the walkway. The juniper branches were so bushy, however, Wil couldn't see who they were.

"Can you believe it?" whispered Sophie.

"What?" asked Wil, who was busy scratching his arm.

"It's the same one," said Sophie.

"The same what?" asked Wil.

"The woman from the honey shop, the one with the black hair."

"Ssssh, or she'll hear you," said Wil, his hands suddenly feeling clammy. Beads of sweat broke out on his forehead as he gingerly moved one of the juniper branches aside.

The woman with the black hair was not ten feet from where he and Sophie were crouched. "You've certainly done a good job of sprucing things up, Madame Non—the outside at least," she said to the other woman, who was wearing a pink suit, which immediately reminded Wil of the colour of a dog's tongue.

"Curb appeal we call it, Mme. Daggar," said the woman in the dog's tongue suit. "I also arranged for a petite interior cleaning. Someone will adore zee 'ouse as soon as zey see it. Zey will be meant for each other."

"Well, buying a house is hardly like falling in love," the woman with the black hair said. "But no house should be without people. I spent my childhood here, you know. But the property has been on the market for years, ever since my grandmother—" She did not finish her sentence.

The woman in the dog's tongue suit did not say anything more, or at least Wil didn't hear her reply, as the two women strolled back to the street.

"So now we know what her last name is," whispered Sophie. "Daggar," she said, emphasizing the second syllable.

"Somehow knowing it sounds like *dagger* doesn't make me feel any better," said Wil, his hands still clammy.

"I know what you mean," said Sophie with a laugh—but it was a small laugh.

"I think they've left," said Wil. "Let's get out of here."

"But we still haven't looked around the back," said Sophie.

Before Wil could say anything, Sophie crept out from under the juniper bush and scampered to the back of the house.

Having no choice but to follow and still scratching his arm, which was covered in nasty red welts, Wil stole around the side of the house. The wind had picked up and dark clouds were now looming overhead. The air suddenly felt chilly. Here and there, the stucco on the house was falling off in great patches. The house looked like it had a bad case of peeling skin from sunburn. Wil was surprised to see the long, unkempt grass at the back of the house was dried out and yellowed. No more spinach green.

Even more surprising, there was a broad swath of brown, murky water snaking past the house. Wil hadn't realized the river was so close to Half Moon Lane. He remembered at the beginning of the school year how the principal at Gruffud's Academy had warned everyone the clock tower and the school lands along the riverbank were off-limits. She had said the waters were treacherous.

The river is slow and sluggish, he thought—hardly something to be afraid of. And even if it is hot, who wants to swim in muddy water anyway? It looks like a cup of Aunt Violet's tea—with too much milk in it.

"Sophie?" he called.

No answer.

"Sophie, this isn't funny," said Wil, looking around anxiously. "If you're hiding, come out *right* now."

Although where Sophie would hide, he had no idea. There were a couple of massive, old twisted willow trees, but the rest of the back yard was empty, except for a ramshackle shed, which had a rusty old padlock on it.

Then he heard Sophie's voice call faintly, "I'm over here."

"I can't see you," said Wil.

"By the river…"

Wil walked cautiously towards the river through the long grasses, glancing behind him nervously.

What if those two women come back and see us, he thought. We'll be in a lot of trouble. And what if Aunt Rue and Aunt Violet are home already and have discovered the empty house? Good-bye Aunt Violet's crullers. Disaster on top of disaster, or would it be a tragedy?

Suddenly, with no warning, his feet slipped right out from under him. With a howl, he rolled down the steep slope of the riverbank.

He opened his eyes to see Sophie's head upside down, her bright eyes peering at him intently as though he were some bizarre insect she'd never encountered before. Her eyeglass frames were now flecked with marbled bits of gold and blue.

"There is a path, you know," she said, and she pointed to a small path leading back up to the house. "Are you trying to let the whole world know we're here? Great spy you'd make."

"Well, if you didn't go wandering—" Will's voice trailed off as he sat up and looked at the river. Lazy bubbles swirled on its surface, and the mud along the riverbanks had cracked into a thousand pieces like the crazy quilts his grandmother used to make. A duck with six ducklings all in a row behind her quacked busily, herding her charges downstream. Hundreds of thistles had already gone to seed; fluffs of thistledown were floating off in the wind.

It was some moments before he realized he had landed on top of a mound of old cardboard boxes, books and bags of clothing.

"What's all this stuff?" he asked.

"I think this is what the woman in the pink suit meant when she said the house was cleaned," said Sophie.

Remembering the house's dark, gloomy interior and the cobwebs, Wil said, "That house was pretty dirty."

"Look what I've got," said Sophie, triumphantly, as she held up something silver.

"What is it?" asked Wil.

"It's an old candlestick—needs some polishing," said Sophie. "And there's a box of old photos here."

There was a rumble of thunder as Sophie handed a dog-eared, stained photograph to Wil.

A young girl and small boy were standing in front of an elderly woman, their grandmother perhaps, thought Wil. He turned the photograph over. The words Lucie, Rufus and Nana were written in spidery writing on the back.

"And here's one of a woman on a beach," said Sophie, holding out another picture. "She's wearing an old-fashioned bathing suit. It's really funny."

This photograph was cracked and the blacks had turned to browns. The young woman was probably in her late teens or early twenties. Across the bottom of the photo in fading brown ink was scrawled *Love, Lucie*.

Wil handed the photographs back to Sophie and picked up several books at random from the pile he was sitting on. The top book was small and seemed to be a diary. The first entry was in large, wobbly printing dated July 20, long ago. He read aloud:

Me and Rufus went to get ice cream store with Nana today. I got one soft vanila cone. Rufus had chocolit wirl but it got sqwashe when it fell in the mud and he was so angry I thought his head was going to fall off his face was turning as red as Nanas nail polish. I love ice cream.

"I wonder who Rufus is," said Wil. "You don't think it's Rufus Crookshank, do you?"

"There can't be too many people named Rufus. It's not a common name. Maybe he was a friend of Lucie's," said Sophie. "And maybe he used to visit here when he was a child."

"That would be really creepy," said Wil, looking back at the house.

"Maybe Lucie, whoever she was, lived here with her grandmother," said Sophie.

Wil felt a shadow fall over him. His heart caught in his throat—and at the same instant, Sophie's frames turned ghost white—as they turned around and saw the woman in the dog's tongue suit.

"*Qu'est-ce que vous faites ici?* Scat, you 'ooligans! You vill be charged with trespassing and stealing. I 'ave 'alf a mind to summon the Firecatchers this instant!"

Although Wil had not understood everything she said—he wasn't sure what ooligan meant—he understood well enough the look of fury on her face. Still clutching two books, his fingers frozen around the bindings, Wil stood up on shaking legs. He tried to think what to say, but his voice was gone.

"We're s-s-sorry," stuttered Sophie. She pointed to the heap of clothing, boxes and books. "We thought all this was g-g-garbage."

"Vell, it is not garbage, and you are definitely trespassing," said the woman in the dog's tongue suit. "Just because dere's a FOR SALE sign doesn't mean you can wander around the property unsupervised. You should not nose into other people's business without taking care of your own first."

With the woman glaring at them both, Wil scampered after Sophie up the steep slope. Large raindrops followed them as they bolted through the long, yellowed grass, across the green grass and ran straight home without stopping once. Panting, they locked the door and collapsed onto the living room floor.

The grandfather's clock gently chimed two o'clock.

"Well, that was fun," said Sophie at last, holding up the silver candlestick, which Wil now saw was in the shape of two dragons. She began to giggle hysterically.

"Almost got ourselves arrested," said Wil, starting to giggle himself. "How did you manage to keep hold of the candlestick? And did you see the expression on her face? I thought we were goners."

Their giggles were cut short, however, when a key rattled in the front door, and Aunt Violet opened the door.

"Such a sudden storm…" she said and she shook the raindrops from her umbrella. "I thought I'd better come home in case you were scared, my dears. Your Aunt Rue had a few more errands and the shop is going to deliver the groceries for us later." She walked into the kitchen and lifted the cover from the crullers. "I can't believe you haven't touched the crullers. What good children. Shall we have some milk and pastries?"

Wil gulped, feeling guilty. He had no right to a cruller and neither did Sophie, for that matter.

Aunt Violet's eyes lit on Wil's lap. "What have you got there?" she asked.

Wil looked down. He'd completely forgotten he was still holding the two books.

"A couple of books one of our neighbours was throwing out," said Sophie quickly. "They were going to get wet, so we rescued them. And we found an old candlestick too." She held out the double-headed candlestick. "It needs a little polishing."

"What interesting finds!" said Aunt Violet and she pounced on the candlestick and books. She seemed to have completely forgotten that Wil and Sophie were supposed to have stayed in the house. "Ridiculous what some people will throw out—perfectly good things," she muttered, as she inspected the candlestick.

Wil leaned forward see what the two books were about. He hadn't even had a chance to open them yet.

First Principles of Managing a Business and *Fortunes' Future.* Boring. What could Aunt Violet possibly want with them? She was still acting strangely and seemed more distracted with each passing day, Wil thought. Her latest project was to sew hundreds of gold stars onto a worn, purple silk tablecloth.

"Such a fine piece of purple fabric with only a few holes to patch—and who will notice with all the gold stars?" she kept saying.

As Wil bit into the cruller drizzled with vipers bugloss honey, he thought...life can't get much better.

X †HE OPEΠ HOUSE

Sssssomething following him was—but what?

SUSPICER VALDE PRATUM VIRIDISSIMUM—ET TU?
I'D BE SUSPICIOUS OF VERY GREEN GRASS, WOULDN'T YOU?

When Sophie and Wil returned the following morning to the house at the end of the street, there were nine lush bouquets of flowers in pots at the front of the house and the grass was greener than ever. Beneath the FOR SALE sign hung another sign, which read OPEN HOUSE

They dashed across the green grass to the side of the house where they had hidden the day before. Wil's feet were soaked from the damp lawn. He bent down to take them off, while Sophie stood on her tiptoes to peer through the window above their heads. She ducked down quickly.

"She's in there," she whispered.

"Who?" asked Wil, shaking off his shoes.

"The woman in the pink suit," said Sophie.

"What's she doing?"

"There are some people with her, and she was pointing at the chandelier."

Wil was about to look in the window himself, when it scraped opened suddenly.

"A truly unusual house with many lovely features," said a voice—it sounded like the woman in the dog's tongue suit. "A large 'ouse to accommodate a growing family. Three full bathrooms, a large walk-in kitchen. Lovely view of the *rivière*. Outstanding value for dis location."

"The neighbourhood is a little rundown," said a man's voice gruffly. "I think we're in the market for something more upscale."

"I can certainly help you find exactly what you are looking for," said the woman in the dog's tongue suit. "Why don't you take my card…"

The voices faded as they stepped away from the window.

"Let's go in," said Sophie.

"Do you think we should?" asked Wil. "That woman must be the real estate agent. She'll kick us out."

"It's a free country, and there's no reason why we shouldn't go in like everybody else," said Sophie.

"I still don't think we should—" said Wil, but Sophie had obviously made up her mind and was already around the corner. Wil sighed and put his soggy shoes back on. As he mounted the front stairs, he passed a man and a woman who were leaving the house. They were both shaking their heads, and the man threw a business card into the bushes.

Wil crept inside the house. Gone were the spider webs from the chandelier; it shone in all its glory, hundreds of crystals sparkling proudly. And gone were the sheets from the stuffed furniture. The house was gleaming, the floors freshly polished. There was even a large bowl of red apples on the table.

Sophie was gazing at one of the portraits on the wall. It was of a severe-looking elderly woman with jet-black hair and pale skin. She was dressed in a long velvet dress with ribbons and ruffles, and was holding a book in her left hand. Wil wondered if she had been the previous owner of the house. Wherever he moved, her eyes seemed to follow him. He shivered a little.

"That painting is creepy," he said. "Do you see how her eyes follow you?"

"All the old paintings do that," said Sophie. "They painted them that way."

"Are you sure?" asked Wil, looking back up at the woman, who definitely appeared to be staring at him, or *through* him was more like it, he thought.

"*Qu'est-ce que vous faites ici?* What are you doing 'ere?" The woman in the dog's tongue suit towered over them in her high-heeled shoes. "Didn't I tell you children to scat yesterday?" she hissed.

At the sound of footsteps coming up the front steps, the woman's face changed expression immediately. She turned around and smiled at a man and woman who were coming in the door.

Wil felt immediately he would like to get to know them. The man had a black ink stain on the middle finger of his left hand and a small frayed notebook peeking out of his pocket. Perhaps he was a writer. Mr. Bertram had told him writers always carried a small notebook with them to jot down ideas so they wouldn't lose them.

The woman was holding a long checklist. "Madame Non?" she said. "So pleased to meet you. This is my husband, Otis Bain."

"But yes, Mr. and Mrs. Bain," exclaimed the woman in the dog's tongue suit. "I'm so glad you both could come."

"Yes, we're just in town for the day," said Mrs. Bain.

"Zis is a beautiful house. A photograph does not do it justice," said the woman in the dog's tongue suit. "It has obviously been well-loved over the years. So many unique features, as you can see. A perfect view of the *rivière*. Three full bathrooms, a large walk-in kitchen. Outstanding value."

"Yes," said Mrs. Bain, as she eyed a large crack in the wall.

I could put my whole hand inside that crack, thought Wil.

"Before you show us the house," said Mrs. Bain, "I have a few questions I'd like to ask you first."

"But of course," said the woman in the dog's tongue suit. "I am 'ere to answer any questions you may 'ave. Please, ask away."

Mrs. Bain consulted her checklist. "To your knowledge, have any of the previous owners died in the house?"

Whatever questions the woman in the dog's tongue suit may have been expecting, this clearly was not one of them. "I do not understand," she said.

"Has anyone died in this house before?" said Mrs. Bain.

"I…I…I'm afraid I do not know the answer," said the woman in the dog's tongue suit.

"I can sense at least one presence here. I have been unable to ascertain its intentions towards the living," said Mrs. Bain matter-of-factly. "I don't suppose it really matters. In my experience, those whose spirits linger have unfinished business. These are things we, the living, can often help with."

"Ah…yes," said the woman in the dog's tongue suit, who for once seemed speechless.

Mrs. Bain glanced down at her checklist again. "Now, when was the last time the river flooded?"

"The river?" repeated the woman in the dog's tongue suit, as if there were no river, and even if there were a river, she wasn't sure what the word meant exactly. "Oh, you mean, the *rivière!*"

"Yes, the *rivière,*" said the woman with her eyebrows arched.

The woman in the dog's tongue suit smiled and waved her hands airily. "The *rivière* has a mind of its own sometimes," she said.

That woman has such a fake smile, thought Wil. He wanted to run over to the man and woman and scream, *Don't trust her!* He felt Sophie's hand on his arm holding him back.

"What?" he said, pulling his arm away from her.

"You look like you're ready to attack the woman in the pink suit," said Sophie.

"No, I don't," said Wil.

"Yes, you do," said Sophie.

The man and woman wandered over to the fireplace to look at the mantle, which was ornately carved with a large mirror above.

The man turned around and asked, "Madame Non, are there lots of children in the neighbourhood?" asked the man, and he glanced over at Wil and Sophie.

The woman in the dog's tongue suit began to say, "I am not aware—"

"We have lots of children of our own, and it would be nice if there were some other children to play with," he continued.

"Why, I believe there are lots of children. This is a very child-friendly street," said the woman in the dog's tongue suit, with a big smile directed in Wil's and Sophie's direction. "And it's not far for them to walk to school either. It's so important to foster children's sense of independence, don't you think? Why don't we take a look upstairs?"

The woman led the couple up the stairs, but not before she glared at Sophie and Wil one last time.

"Can you believe her?" asked Wil.

Sophie shook her head.

"Do you think this house will ever sell?" asked Wil, thinking he'd never buy a house from the woman in the dog's tongue suit.

❖❖❖❖❖❖

Sophie and Wil had just finished a bed-time snack of hot chocolate and biscuits when Aunt Rue came in the door.

"Children, I'm sorry to be so late, but I do have some good news," said Aunt Rue, as she plopped her briefcase on the kitchen table.

"I kept your supper warm for you," said Aunt Violet. "Why so late, Rue?"

"Another meeting, Aunt Violet. I'm really sorry," said Aunt Rue. "But before the good news, I have a little something for you, Sophie."

Sophie's eyes lit up in anticipation, but her face fell when she saw what it was.

"I'm sure this will work," said Aunt Rue, and she held out a small bottle labelled *Happy Hands*.

Sophie reluctantly took the bottle from Aunt Rue. Merrily Klimchak had told her about *Happy Hands*; her mother had forced her to use it. According to Merrily, the stuff was a revolting colour of orange and smelled really foul. And it tasted worse.

"What's that?" asked Wil.

"Oh, something special to help Sophie's fingernails grow," said Aunt Rue brightly. She looked expectantly at Sophie.

"Thank you, Aunt Rue," said Sophie without any enthusiasm.

"So, tell us the news, Rue," said Aunt Violet.

"Well, I get to go to an international bee conference in England."

"You mean people from all over the world are going to be talking about bees?" asked Sophie, trying to imagine what it would be like to have hundreds of beekeepers in one big room together.

"All the bee experts in the world will be gathered in one place," said Aunt Rue. "We'll be able to learn from each other's work. And I've heard that people attending the conference bring honey with them. I think I'll take some buckwheat honey with me, as that's one of our local specialties."

Sophie's tongue shrivelled at the mere thought of the buckwheat honey.

"Wonderful news, Rue," said Aunt Violet. "Congratulations! They must really like the work you've been doing. When are you going?"

"Towards the middle of August," said Aunt Rue. "Time to get ready for bed, children. Skedaddle, the both of you. And before I forget, I did get in touch with Mage Radix and you can go visit him next week."

Sophie clapped her hands. "Thank you, Aunt Rue!"

Sophie started to follow Wil up the stairs but paused, as she heard Aunt Rue say, "I don't know, Aunt Violet. There's something odd going on."

"Wil, wait," she whispered and tugged at his pant leg.

Wil turned around quickly and looked down at her questioningly.

"Ssshhh," she said. "Listen."

"Maybe by sending me to the conference, they're just trying to get rid of me," said Aunt Rue. "Just when I'm potentially on the verge of a breakthrough. I don't know what's going on, but the Deputy Minister herself has been going through my data. And some of my research has been taken and published—without my name even being given any credit."

"What!" exclaimed Aunt Violet. "That's not right."

"I don't know what to do," said Aunt Rue. "She's top-notch in the field, even if we don't get along. But she seems to have changed or something—she's different. She's always looking over my shoulder. I have the feeling they're going to assign me to another department...or worse. I can't lose this job. Where would we be then? It's been ten years, Aunt Violet, ten long years of living under the shadow of Cyril's disappearance."

"But ten good years too, Rue. Think of the children. They're growing so well."

The clattering of dishes ended the conversation, sending Sophie and Wil up the stairs.

"Didn't sound good, did it?" whispered Sophie.

"Not good is an understatement. I'd say it's really serious," whispered Wil. "We've got to do something."

"But what?" asked Sophie, her mind spinning. How to make sense of it all? The MiddleGate bees falling sick, the *apiponis destructor*, the mysterious honey, that black-haired Daggar woman, whoever she was, plus the threat of Aunt Rue losing her job.

"Do you think Portia and Portius will know what's wrong with the bees?" she said finally. "They always seem to know what to do."

"We can try asking them when we go to see Mage Radix next week," whispered Wil. "And I'll write a letter to Mr. Bertram tonight. Maybe he can help."

⚜⚜⚜⚜⚜⚜

After a final goodnight to Esme, Wil pulled out a clean piece of paper and a pen. He sat chewing on the pen for a long while, wondering what to tell Mr. Bertram first.

Half Moon Lane, MiddleGate   *July 7*

Dear Mr. Bertram:

I hope you are well. Esme is resting a lot and doesn't want to eat her eggs. Sophie and I went to the honey shop to get honey for Aunt Violet's pastries. We got some delishus honey called vipers booclose. Isn't that a funny name for honey? It sounds like a snake I think. It's from New Zealand. But what's really strange is there was some kind of strange honey Sophie saw, I didn't see it and it had red strekes in it. There was a woman at the shop who said there is not enough honey but the bee shop seemed to have lots. No one knows why all the bees are getting sick here. Aunt Rue is working so many hours at the S.S.M.C. all the time we hardly ever see her. She is woried about everything. Aunt Violet is reading our tea leaves all the time and now she is sewing a thousand gold stars on a big pirple cloth. We are going to help Mage Radix next week with the bees at Gruffud's. It was Sophie's idea I'm not sure I want to. Olin told us a story about a boy in France who died from one thousand bee stings. I feel sorry for that boy. But Aunt Rue thinks it's a good idea I guess. She spoke to Mage Radix. Ther is something strange going on with the bees here. Do you have any bee books?

Yours sincerly,

Wil

p.s. Sophie and I have an excellent idea. Since the libary needs a libarian we think you should come live in MiddleGate and be the new libarian. We hope you like the idea.

At the prospect of Mr. Bertram coming to live in MiddleGate, Wil was too excited to go to sleep. He pulled out a new book he had found on the shelves in the living room, *The 1001 Tales of Abuuhchnazzar.*

As always, he turned to a page part-way through the book to read it—without having any idea about what was going on. Only then would he start the book from the beginning…and later on…when he came to that page again, he would enjoy how much more he knew about the whole story and all its characters.

He knew Sophie always liked to cruise through the table of contents first. And she could never stop reading in the middle of chapter; she always had to finish a chapter first before putting the book down.

Aunt Rue didn't seem to read much, other than the reports she brought home from work. And when Wil had asked Aunt Violet how she liked to read books, she laughed and told him she always liked to read the end first, then she started back at the beginning. Wil thought that would take the surprise away. Perhaps that was why Aunt Violet was always trying to predict the future, so she'd know the ending of the story first.

But life is different than a book, because a book ends, he thought. Life just keeps going on and on and on. The story never ends.

Wil had opened the book to page 111. There was a picture of a small snake coiling around the stone foot of an enormous statue.

Slithering through the darkness, the young snake known as Silenus paused, his tongue sniffing the air.

Sssssomething following him was—but what?

Swiftly the young snake coiled around the towering stone foot of Abuuhchnazzar's statue and darted into the ear of the severed stone head resting by the foot.

"Sssssilenus," hissed Slissa, the eldest of the Old Snakes, "discover what did you—"

❖·❖·❖·❖·❖·❖

The book slipped from Wil's fingers and fell to the floor. Wil was fast asleep. He dreamt he was being chased by something dangerous—what it was, he didn't know. He only knew he had to escape. He crawled up the massive stone foot at the base of Abuuhchnazzar's statue...

XI Aunt Violet's
Wish Come True

Before their eyes, it began to grow larger.

SAEPE RES NON SUNT QUAE PRIMO ASPECTU VIDENTUR.
THINGS ARE NOT ALWAYS WHAT THEY SEEM AT FIRST GLANCE.

The following evening at the dinner table, Aunt Violet set down an enormous bowl of mashed potatoes on the kitchen table, as Sophie rattled on excitedly.

"Aunt Violet, there were a couple of people looking at that big, old creepy house down the street—the one that's for sale," she said. She stopped to take a big bite of mashed potato. "A really nice man and woman came. They said they liked children."

"What, dear?" asked Aunt Violet, sounding preoccupied. "I can't understand a word you're saying with your mouth full of potato."

Sophie swallowed the potato. "And the grass was so green, it looked really fake."

"That real estate agent must have done something to it," said Wil.

"Perhaps so," said Aunt Violet, looking up at the grandfather's clock. She shooed away Cadmus, who was pawing at a dangly thread hanging from her skirt.

"Do you know who used to live in that house, Aunt Violet?" asked Wil.

"Hmm, dear?" said Aunt Violet.

"Who used to live in the house?" repeated Wil.

"Oh, that house has been derelict for years, children," said Aunt Violet. "Ever since we've been living here and probably long before that."

Aunt Violet glanced at the grandfather's clock again. It was one minute to seven. She had eaten hardly anything on her plate.

"Is someone coming?" asked Sophie.

"Why, snakes alive, what do you mean, Sophie?" asked Aunt Violet, poking at the cold mashed potato on her plate.

Scarcely had Aunt Violet spoken when there was a loud knock on the door. At the same moment, the clock began to chime seven bells.

Aunt Violet jumped up. "Serpent's breath, now who could that be?" she asked.

Her question was answered by the slam of the door as it burst open.

Cadmus flew under the sofa.

In the doorway stood a tall, gangly young man dressed in shimmering silver robes, which were much too large for him. He was holding a silver metal briefcase. As the young man's eyes glanced around the house, Sophie had the distinct impression he was taking in the mismatched furniture in the living room, their half-eaten mash…and the gaping hole in the floor—still not fixed after Aunt Rue's experiment with *One-Shot No-Spot Cleaning Powder* had eaten a hole right through the linoleum.

Aunt Violet stared at him speechless.

"Do I have the right place?" asked the young man. He bowed to Aunt Violet. "You *are* Madam Violet Isidor?"

"Oh, oh yes," said Aunt Violet, and she hastily dabbed her mouth with a serviette. "Do come in. Ah, Mr. Bress?"

"Yes, Odd Bress, but you can call me Odd. Hope I'm not late."

What would it be like to have an odd name like Odd? Sophie thought. She almost burst out laughing. Wil must have been thinking the same thing, because he looked as if he were trying to stifle a giggle himself.

"No, no, not at all," said Aunt Violet, who still seemed to be tongue-tied. "And, I hope it's all right if the two children watch your presentation, Mr. Br—I mean, Odd," asked Aunt Violet.

"No prob," replied the young man, and he swooped into the living room and placed the briefcase on the sofa.

What presentation? thought Sophie. She tiptoed over to the briefcase, and as the young man opened it, she leaned forward to see what was inside.

It was filled with exquisite, shiny glass marbles of every hue imaginable.

Why is Aunt Violet interested in marbles? thought Sophie.

"Take a jiffy to set up," said the young man. "Make yourselves comfortable. Thank you for inviting me to give this presentation, Madam Isidor.

"Perfect Products Inc. is always pleased to showcase its classic goods and new developments in the field. As you may know, we have been in the business of serving our customers for five hundred and seventy-four years—no mean feat these days with every fly-by-night company attempting to import inferior copies of our products… preying on unsuspecting customers. But where are they when you need them? Here today, gone tomorrow.

"But not Perfect Products. Our reputation resides in the quality of our products, our service and our top-of-the-line lifetime guarantee."

Classic products, new developments, top-of-the-line? What was he talking about? Sophie glanced at Aunt Violet, who seemed to be transfixed by the marbles in the briefcase.

The young man chose the largest clear marble from the briefcase. He held the marble up to the light. It shimmered like rippling water on a summer's day. He placed the marble in the palm of his left hand and blew upon it.

The tiny ball shivered; before their eyes, it began to grow larger.

Now it was as big as an orange…a moment later, it was as big as a grapefruit.

The young man smiled and blew on it again.

The marble swelled as large as a round watermelon. The young man stepped back and the shining glass orb remained suspended in front of Aunt Violet.

"Beautiful, isn't she?" said the young man, as he whipped out a fluffy, green polishing cloth and removed an invisible spot of dust from the orb. "This is a quality product—unrivalled, as far as I'm concerned. One of the reasons I love this job...Perfect Products Inc. makes beautiful things. Everyone we show loves them, and that's why they are so popular. And you can take advantage of our fine trade-in programme, if you'd like to turn in one of your old crystal ball models. We'd be happy to give you a generous discount off your new purchase for substantial overall savings."

Aunt Violet nodded her head, seemingly hypnotized by the ball, which quivered before her—as though eager for Aunt Violet to touch it.

"But Aunt Violet, you don't have any crystal balls," said Sophie.

"I see," said the young man, with a sharp glance at Sophie. "Well, this certainly is one of our most popular orbs—the *Princess* line. Note its shimmering translucidity, scarcely a bubble to disrupt the true-to-life highest resolution image. Perfectly spherical. Guaranteed for past and future prognistications. Silky smooth. Rare glass, precision manufacture straight from our Icelandic factory. No impurities. Polished to the highest possible degree with current geothermal technologies. You won't find its equal anywhere, I vouch. Guaranteed not to smoke or cloud unduly.

"And it comes, of course, with the best in security features. Can be set so only its owner—you, Madam Isidor—may use it. It has a password protect; fingerprint, iris-check and voice-check; screech alarm; and self-destruct option as well, depending on your needs."

A *real* crystal ball! So this is why Aunt Violet has been so secretive, thought Sophie. Sophie leaned over to stare into the orb but saw nothing except her own reflection.

Wil peered inside too, but he must have jostled the ball, for it jerked away, as if angry at being bumped. Wil stepped back, looking shaken.

"Gentle there. One at a time, please," said the young man. "Sorry, kids. The Princess is superbly balanced and must be treated with care. Without special training, by the way, you will see only your own reflection."

"Wil, careful, please," said Aunt Violet. "Ah, I'm not sure we need something quite so elaborate, you know…" Her voice trailed off.

"Yes, fair enough, I understand," said the young man, undeterred by Aunt Violet's hesitation. "Fair enough—for small-scale domestic or commercial use, of course, I understand completely.

"Perfect Products has a number of lines to interest you, as I know you're set on becoming an owner of one—and perhaps more than one—of our "perfect products"! Why don't we take a look at the *Rose*?"

As before, the young man took out a marble from the briefcase, this one as pale pink as one of Aunt Violet's powder puffs.

"Yes, the lovely *Rose* model. Clear, reliable images. Not with the true-to-life, three-dimensional qualities associated with the *Princess*, of course. But then the price is right. The slight rose-coloured cast you see inclines to the optimistic. In our experience, many customers prefer this tint over our darker models. I could offer you this *Rose* ball together with a set of active prisms ready-to-use."

"And how much does the *Rose* cost?" asked Aunt Violet.

"I can tell you really appreciate what Perfect Products has to offer," said the young man. "And you're so lucky. The *Rose* is actually this week's *Featured Promotion* for our special customers," he boasted. "It's a real deal—I'd buy it myself if I were in the market for one. You can't sell a product you don't believe in yourself. So, yes, the prisms… and it comes with a real Certificate of Authenticity; mail-in rebate; and complete instructions for use in ten different languages."

"I'm…I'm not sure—" said Aunt Violet.

"And just for you, Madam Isidor," interrupted the young man, "we can throw in a complimentary cleaning cloth; special oak stand engraved with your choice of five words; plus a unique set of glass earrings, necklace and bracelet together with anklet. The carrying case would be an extra, of course."

Aunt Violet nodded and said, "Perhaps I'll think about—"

"Just compare our competitors' prices," said the young man, and he whipped out a list from his robes and pointed to a long column of numbers. "Yes, here's the *Rose* model from Perfect Products Inc., and the price for a comparable item produced by one of our close competitors, Mangel's Glass Balls—you can see for yourself—ours is two-thirds the price," he said, triumph on his face, as if Aunt Violet had no choice but to purchase the *Rose* on the spot.

Aunt Violet flinched as she read the list. Sophie leaned over Aunt Violet's shoulder to look at it, but the young man quickly whipped it from Aunt Violet's hands and pocketed it. From the dismay on Aunt Violet's face, the ball must have cost an astronomical sum.

The young man seemed not to notice, however, and proceeded to pull out marble after marble, until the living room was filled with luminescent orbs floating mid-air, some clear like the *Princess* and the *Rose*; others glowing a deep ruby colour or shimmering emerald.

Cadmus's eyes gleamed from underneath the sofa where he still lay hidden; unblinking, he watched the orbs glowing above his head.

"Ah, Mr. Odd...perhaps one of your demonstration models is available?" asked Aunt Violet. "Or do you have a slightly flawed ball that needs a good home? Perhaps a second-hand one?"

The young man looked disappointed. But his face brightened a moment later. "Fair enough. You surely drive a hard bargain, Madam Isidor, but I have no doubt we can come to some agreement. I just happen to have here a lovely little ball—known as the *BUZzz*—intimate, manageable for the busy witch or wizard and eminently portable, more than sufficient for your needs, I'm sure. A beautiful little piece. The last one. I've been saving it for that special customer, and I think we've just found her!"

The young man pulled out the last marble from the briefcase—a tiny, black marble. He rubbed it on the sleeve of his robe.

"This is one of our recently discontinued lines, but the *BUZzz* was always one of my personal favourites. Don't know why they aren't making it any more actually. Many of our customers liked the name, you know. The *BUZzz* does vibrate or hum a little. Lovely quality, reminds one of crystal night. Just like ordinary glass, isn't it? But it's actually obsidian, black volcanic crystal—renowned for its sometimes grisly predictions—not everyone's up for such acute detail perhaps. They do say bad news travels fast, don't they?

"This little buzzing beauty is perfectly spherical, well, almost. Now, I will warn you the slightly pitted surface in one sector reflects its Icelandic volcanic origins, of course——that's part of its power— and a minute, practically invisible, scarcely noticeable crack—well, hardly worth mentioning really, is it?"

The young man paused to take a breath, and Sophie wondered how he could possibly speak so quickly.

Aunt Violet touched the *BUZzz* gingerly. Golden sparks shot out and the orb practically flew into her hands. A distinct humming, purring sound emanated from it.

"It seems to have found its owner," said the young man. "That's settled then." And before Aunt Violet could say another word, he whipped out a contract.

"Sign here...monthly payments of twenty doublers...lifetime guarantee—no, we'll have to scratch that one out, won't we... instructions—sorry, I don't have those, but I'll get the office to send you a copy...ah, what else, just sign here on this line please."

By the time Aunt Violet had signed her name at the bottom of the contract, all the orbs had dimmed, shrunk back to the size of marbles and were neatly stashed in the silver briefcase. The living room seemed dark and empty, but for the single, glowing *BUZzz* ball still resting in Aunt Violet's hands.

"Don't worry about me. I can see myself to the door," said the young man. "No trouble at all. A pleasure meeting you. Certainly look forward to working with you in the future.

"Oh, and before I forget, here is your Perfect Products *Official Chance Entry Form*. All Perfect Products Inc. customers are eligible to enter our famous draw held once a year in the spring. First prize a *Mystery Trip* for two adults and two children. Just fill out the entry form in duplicate and mail one copy to our office. Don't forget to fill in the reference number from your contract—ACE-0Y-12357-11131719," he said, squinting down at the contract. "You'll answer a skill-testing question if your name is drawn, and make sure you don't lose your copy of the contract or you won't be eligible to win."

With that, the young man's robes swirled out the door and he was gone.

Cadmus crawled out from underneath the sofa. He sniffed at the still humming ball nestled in Aunt Violet's lap and then darted from the room.

"That young man certainly was full of energy. And with such a curious name too. Odd Bress," said Aunt Violet, looking stunned, as if she couldn't believe her own good fortune. "I wonder what got into Cadmus."

"He's scared of the *BUZzz* ball. It's bigger than he is!" said Sophie, as she pounced on the pink *Official Chance Entry Form,* which the young man had left on the table. "Wouldn't it be amazing if we won the draw, Aunt Violet?"

"I wouldn't get your hopes up, dear," said Aunt Violet as she ran her hand lovingly over the black *BUZzz.* "Think of how many people must order things from Perfect Products."

"I don't care," said Sophie, clutching the entry form.

"These numbers on the contract are prime numbers," said Wil. "Remember Mage Adderson told us in numeristics prime numbers are powerful because they can only be divided by the number one and by themselves." In his excitement, he blurted out the words all in one breath.

Aunt Violet seemed taken aback, then she smiled. "Maybe you're right, children. With such numbers, we may get lucky!" Her smile faded. "By serpent's grace, you won't tell Aunt Rue about the *BUZzz,* will you?" she said, lowering her voice and looking embarrassed. "She'll think I've gone scaly. But I've always wanted one of these things; it's a wish come true."

"Don't worry, Aunt Violet," said Wil.

"We won't tell, as long as you stop making us drink tea so you can read the leaves," said Sophie with a grin, thinking she had never seen Aunt Violet look so happy.

"I had no idea crystal balls were so expensive," said Aunt Violet, her arms wrapped around the black *BUZzz.* "And no more tea, I promise."

XII THE BOOK OF QUAERIES

A book of blank pages.

SI DE FUTURIS QUAERIMUS
VIDENDUM EST UTRUM RESPONSUM
NOBIS PLACEAT ANNON.
WE CAN ASK ABOUT THE FUTURE,
BUT THE ANSWER MAY—OR MAY NOT—
PLEASE US.

The comforting, musty smell of old book bindings filled the air. Comics jostled scientific tomes, and yellowed maps elbowed well-thumbed dictionaries. Juicy novels and genealogies spanning hundreds of years competed for shelf space with children's books.

Mr. Bertram always resented calling them *children's* books, as though no one else could learn anything from them or enjoy them.

"So…now what, Mr. Pirsstle?" he asked.

But as Mr. Bertram was the only one in Pirsstle and Bertram's Antiquarian Booksellers—his partner Mr. Pirsstle had died many years ago—merely the squeaky silence of shelves swarming with books greeted his question. Ever since Wil had left Toronto for MiddleGate after the death of his grandmother (she had lived in one of the apartments above Pirsstle and Bertram's for many years and took

Wil in when both his parents died)—Mr. Bertram had been talking to himself quite a bit. And now he had even taken to conversing with the late Mr. Pirsstle.

How can I find a book, if I don't know where to look for it? young Wil had always asked Mr. Bertram.

But Mr. Bertram would only smile and say, *We all make order from chaos. Do not worry. The book will find you, Wil.*

Mr. Bertram pulled out a small brass key from his pocket and opened the oak cabinet of miniature books. He found what he was looking for—*The Book of Quaeries.* A tattered blue book, no larger than the palm of his hand. A book of blank pages.

The last time he had consulted the book was on some trifling matter of love.

But that was long ago, thought Mr. Bertram.

"Miss that boy," he murmured. "A shame his grandmother died in the fire. It's not safe here now, Mr. Pirsstle."

He cradled the shabby blue book in his hands, closed his eyes, traced the double-headed serpent coiled on the cover with his finger.

Three times clockwise.

Three times counter-clockwise…just as one should.

The Book of Quaeries trembled in his hands. Tendril wisps of smoke eddied out from the book and circled around him.

He took a deep breath.

Eyes still closed, he opened the book, exhaled slowly.

The smoken, serpentine fingers slipped back into the pages of the book with a sighing sound.

He opened his eyes.

And there, on the page, scrawled in ink as red as pomegranate juice, appeared one word.

LEAVES

What was that supposed to mean?

Mr. Bertram sighed. As usually happened with such magical messages, this one was certainly on the hazy side.

Did the message refer to the leaves of a book, the leaves of some ancient tree, or did it mean he should leave?

XIII Seven Beehives

Mage Radix took down a strange container from the shelf.

UMBRAS AMANT SICUT LUMEN.
THEY LOVE SHADOWS JUST AS THEY LOVE LIGHT.

Wil awoke with a start and a gnawing sense of nervousness. It took him a moment to remember why.

The beehives, he thought. Today is the day we're going to the Gruffud's beehives. He rolled over and groaned.

❖❖❖❖❖❖

"Let's go see Portia and Portius first," said Sophie, as they walked past the Brimstone Snakes in Grunion Square. "Then we'll go over to the greenhouse and meet Mage Radix."

The Gruffud's school grounds were completely deserted; it was eerie seeing no teachers and students about. Mr. and Mrs. Pyper, the school caretakers, had obviously been busy, however, for the tile floors inside the foyer were gleaming and the smells of wax and polish filled the air.

As usual, Portia and Portius, the two stone heads atop Gruffud's entranceway column, were involved in some deep philosophical discussion. This one must have been more intense than usual, for Portia's long stone snake braids were actually hissing at Portius, while the snakes in his stony beard writhed and their tongues lashed the air.

"Portia, Portia, clearly we are at odds with each other—" said Portius.

"Yet again, Portius," interrupted Portia. "But it seems obvious to me the quality of black is at issue here. It is not simply enough for a shadow to be black. The more interesting question is how dark is the shadow?"

"I still think how sharp the edges are determines the shadow's true strength," replied Portius.

"How do they find new things to say about shadows after 494 years?" Wil whispered to Sophie. "And don't they ever get sick of one another's company?"

Portia and Portius broke off when they realized Sophie and Wil were standing right there.

"Our summer greetings, Miss Isidor and Mr. Wychwood," said Portia, her snake braids waving in the air at them. "A pleasure to see you so soon."

"The summer months are always quiet," said Portius, his beard now smooth but for one stone snake that stared curiously at them.

"Yes, we have time to think, to contemplate—" said Portia.

"To argue—" said Portius.

"—and to discuss," said Portia, correcting him. "We take advantage of the opportunity to discuss the finer points of our existence and purpose. Thank the stars above that the Firecatchers are gone now. Mage Agassiz is no doubt pleased she is able to conduct her duties as Principal without bumping into those wretched—" but Portia obviously couldn't think of a word to describe the Firecatchers sufficiently.

Wil could sympathize with Portia. He too had not enjoyed the presence of the Firecatchers. After Wil had been kidnapped by the Snake in the Grass himself, Rufus Crookshank—and in an effort to quell the uproar over students' safety—Mage Radix had been forced to have the Firecatchers posted at the school. The Firecatchers wore long red cloaks, which obscured their faces, and they always gave Wil the uneasy feeling they were probing his mind, trying to force him to reveal things he did not want them to know. An imperceptible cloud of smoke eddied about them; it left you feeling muddled and confused. Even Portia and Portius had been reduced to singing lullabies one day, after being questioned by the Firecatchers.

"You know we shall never agree on the subject of the Firecatchers, my dear Portia—nor upon many other subjects, dare I say," said Portius.

"The children's safety was paramount."

Portia sniffed, making it clear she still felt insulted the Firecatchers had been called in—casting in doubt Portia's and Portius's integrity and commitment to Gruffud's Academy, its teachers and students.

"We're helping Mage Radix today," said Sophie, interrupting them. "We heard some of the bees are getting sick."

'We thought you would know why, if anyone did," said Wil.

"We are honoured you hold our knowledge in such high regard," said Portius.

"But remember, ours is the knowledge of human frailty and the ineffable patterns of nature—" said Portia.

"—not the mere dull narration of human (and other) facts," said Portius.

"Bees love the light. Each droplet of their honeyed nectar breathes sunlight," mused Portia, "yet their hives are dark, redolent with the most fragrant beeswax, bathed in darkest shadows."

"The creatures love the warm shadows as they do the light," said Portius.

"Wise creatures. Have they not been known to swarm before the death of their keeper?"

Wil wondered what the word swarm meant, but Portia and Portius began to chant before he could ask:

If we were you—but we are not
Should you yourself not ask a bee
If she is truly and sincerely free?

"But how are we supposed to talk to bees?" asked Sophie. "I mean, they don't understand English or French or Inuktitut or Mandarin or

Japanese or Icelandic—"

"Not to mention *we* don't speak *Bee-Tongue*, if there is such a thing!" exclaimed Wil, as he bent two fingers to make antennae on top of his head.

Portius and Portia laughed at Wil's expression, but their voices were serious:

Where there's a will (and a Wil you bee!),
there is a way we cannot see.
But the merry bees will be provoked;
we guarantee this is no joke.

They'd not exactly answered Sophie's question, thought Wil.

✦✦✦✦✦✦

Mage Radix was waiting for them in the greenhouse, which looked like a grand glass palace filled with plants and trees. Some, like the banana trees, towered to the top of the dome.

Mage Radix, a broad-shouldered man who taught botanicals, was as stout as he was tall. Wil had hardly ever seen him without a plant in his hand. He talked to the plants, stroked them, played music for them and Wil wouldn't have been surprised if he woke up in the middle of the night to take care of an ailing plant. His love of plants was so great he had even named some of them. *Katarina*, a snake plant with leathery, sword-like leaves, had been in his family for sixty-seven years.

"Your Aunt Rue is a persuasive woman," said Mage Radix, as he greeted them with a hearty laugh. "Made me promise you'd wear your bee suits while you're here. They'll protect you from getting stung. So, follow me."

Mage Radix led them both to a shed filled with wooden boxes piled high to the ceiling, along with frames, shovels, hoses, pans, dippers, strainers and spoons. On the wall was a poster with large letters emblazoned across it.

DRAGONFLY FESTIVAL

71

A dragonfly with sparkling wings swooped across the poster, looking for all the world like a fairy child.

Mage Radix saw Wil and Sophie gazing at the poster. "You two going to the Dragonfly Festival at Bird's Hill?" he asked. "Just two weeks away. Better get your tickets fast before they're all sold out."

"It looks amazing," said Sophie.

"A great festival," said Mage Radix. "You wouldn't believe how many dragonflies there are. There's a honey booth too. And if you're lucky, you'll see the man with a bee beard."

"A bee beard?" asked Wil. "What's a bee beard look like?'

"You'll just have to come to the festival to find out, won't you?" replied Mage Radix, with a smile. "The fellow has a queen bee in a small box around his neck—she releases her special pheromone or queenly smell—and all the other bees follow her. Think of thousands of bees, each one with six feet, and they're all hanging on for dear life to the man's skin, his shirt or whatever else. Bet it tickles." He laughed. "Now, we'll get you all suited up." He rummaged around in a big wooden chest in the corner of the shed and pulled out two pairs of small white coveralls. "You can put these bee suits right over what you're wearing."

Wil had imagined a bee suit would have yellow and black stripes. Sophie must have been expecting the same thing because the frames of her eyeglasses were yellow streaked with black.

Mage Radix saw the disappointment on their faces. "Bet you thought a bee suit was going to be yellow and black, didn't you? Many do," he said with a grin. "But the bees like the white suits. They might think you're a big, black bear about to ransack their nest if you wear black. Remember, you've got to think like a bee when you're a beekeeper. The bees have their likes and dislikes, just as we humans do. And if I were a bee come to visit, I'd bring a little nectar or pollen as a gift. Don't arrive empty-handed—or empty-legged, if you're a bee with a pollen basket, as the case may be—or the bees won't like that." Mage Radix laughed as he said this.

"Think like a bee," whispered Wil to himself, as he wrestled into the coveralls. He was tickled to see Sophie's frames had suddenly become milky white.

"Bees are happy and humming on a day like today," said Mage Radix, as he continued to rummage around in the chest. "Nice, sunny day. The ladies will be buzzy-busy out foraging for nectar. They'll turn churlish on a rainy day though. Best not open a hive on a rainy day.

"And speaking of hives, thought you may be interested in seeing this." Mage Radix pointed to a large, cone-shaped wicker container, with a small round hole at the bottom. "This is what the beehives used to look like—it's called a skep. We don't use them anymore, although I like the look of them myself."

"I like it," said Sophie, running her hand over the wicker braids. "Why aren't they used anymore?"

"Hives nowadays are wooden boxes," replied Mage Radix. "They have individual rectangular frames inside—easier to take the frames out when you're harvesting the honey. The combs can be put back in their place like a book being returned to the shelf."

"Here we are," Mage Radix said triumphantly, as he held out two pairs of long leather gloves and two broad-brimmed white helmets covered in netting.

"What are those for?" asked Wil, who was still struggling to get into his coveralls.

"You'll be covered head to toe, so no stings," said Mage Radix and he handed the gloves and helmets to each of them.

"Don't you wear these too?" asked Wil.

"Oh, no, not after years of working with the bees. They're used to me and I'm used to them. We have an understanding."

"Mage Radix, we heard there's something wrong with the bees," said Sophie, as she tried on the gloves, which went all the way to her elbows. "Some of them are getting sick. We heard there's something called an *apiponis destructor.*"

"Never heard of it." asked Mage Radix. "Sounds like some made-up name to give children bad dreams. Lots of other things to get the bees, though," he said sadly. "Wax moths eat out the walls of a bee city. Skunks and raccoons love their honey, and eat the bee larvae and sometimes even the bees themselves. Colonies collapse. Mites too, those tiny parasites we can't see. At least we don't have bears here. Just fungus, chalkbrood, foulbrood and other awful things. Terrible thing to hit a hive, that foulbrood. You can smell it right away…it's a foul stink, the smell of death's rot. Young, healthy brood—beautiful, glowing bits of life—decompose into globs of sticky, black goo practically before your eyes."

At the look of horror on Sophie's face, Mage Radix ended his grisly description. "But don't worry your heads about those things. Only your first day, after all!" he exclaimed.

"But we heard there are other things going on," Wil said, although he couldn't imagine worse things than Mage Radix had already described. He was about to tell Mage Radix what he and Sophie had managed to cobble together, but Sophie gave him a warning look. Instead, Wil finished doing up the snaps on his coveralls.

"All those things aren't enough?" asked Mage Radix. "You two always on the lookout for trouble?" Mage Radix was obviously joking, but his eyes clouded over as he spoke.

Wil and Sophie clapped the white helmets onto their heads and pulled the netting down over their necks.

It was hot under the helmet, but Wil felt much safer from the bees underneath the netting, even if he couldn't see quite as well.

"Good fit," said Mage Radix. "You can take those helmets off for just a moment. Got a little job for you to do first. After that, we'll introduce you to the bees and you can help clean some of the equipment."

Mage Radix took down a strange container from the shelf. It looked like a metal cookie box with a round spout, but had another accordion box attached to it. He pulled the lid off the cookie box. "This is a bee smoker," he said. "We'll put some burlap scraps in the box and dried grass, then light it. Pop the lid back on the box and it's ready to go. The smoke will help calm the bees."

He handed some small strips of burlap to Sophie and Wil. "Stuff them in the bottom there. Now, who wants to light the match?"

Wil suddenly felt faint and dizzy; he shook his head.

Sophie eagerly took the box from Mage Radix and struck one of the matches on the side of the box.

The match burst into flame. Mesmerized, Wil watched, his breathing laboured. The flame flickered white-blue, then orange. It seemed to grow larger and larger, until Wil could see nothing else… but…the…flame.

"Good," said Mage Radix encouragingly. "Just hold it inside the box until the burlap lights."

Sophie held the match steady then dropped it into the box, as a slow curl of smoke spiralled into the air.

Wil took a deep breath. It was all right. It was only a little match. Nothing to be scared of, he told himself.

Mage Radix stuffed dried grass in the box and snapped the lid down. "Mr. Wychwood, why don't you pump the bellows?"

"The what?" asked Wil.

"The bellows. That's what this other accordion box is for," said Mage Radix. "The bellows bring fresh air into the box to feed the fire."

Wil squeezed the bellows once, feebly.

"You can put a bit more elbow into it, my boy," said Mage Radix. "Here, I'll show you."

He pumped the bellows vigorously, and the spout of the smoker belched a puff of smoke.

"There, ready to go," said Mage Radix. "You can put your helmets and gloves on now."

Mage Radix strode across the field near the greenhouse towards a series of stacked wooden boxes Wil had never noticed before.

"Are those the beehives?" Wil asked.

"All seven of them," said Mage Radix, "in a snaky zigzag pattern. Helps the bees find their home hive. You've got to make sure the hives face south; they've got to have some shade too. They're close to the small woods here, and the river's not too far for them to get water."

"What's that beehive there?" asked Sophie, pointing to the middle of the hive, "The one with the red stripe."

"The stripe helps the bees navigate home," said Mage Radix.

Mage Radix's eyes shifted a little as he said this, thought Wil—as if he were thinking of something else, but not saying it.

"But the other hives all have a black stripe on them," said Sophie.

"I probably just ran out of black paint at the time," said Mage Radix. "My, you've got sharp eyes, Miss Isidor. Had a spot of trouble with that hive. They swarmed."

There was that word swarm again, thought Wil. He still didn't know what it meant.

At the look of puzzlement on Sophie's and Wil's faces, Mage Radix said, "Bees won't generally swarm before a storm. But for some reason, several thousand of those bees took off one morning to find a new nest just before a sudden thunderstorm. Lost every single one of them. When they take off like that, it's called swarming."

"Where did they go?" asked Sophie.

"Bees have a mind of their own," said Mage Radix, without answering Sophie's question.

"Why did they leave?" asked Wil.

"Oftentimes, it's because the nest is too crowded or the queen is old," said Mage Radix. "They're not happy for some reason."

"Then it's a good thing to find a new place to live, right?" asked Wil.

"Yes and no," said Mage Radix slowly. "Depends." He pumped a little smoke into the hole in the lid of the hive closest to them and pried off the lid with a small metal hive tool.

A sweet smell filled Wil's nostrils and the sound of bees buzzing grew louder as the lid lifted.

Mage Radix pumped more smoke into the hive. "Smoke distracts and calms the bees, so they won't fuss when we visit them," he said. "When they smell the smoke, they eat as much honey as they can, in case there's a fire and they have to leave the hive."

Wil had never seen so many bees in one place. There were hundreds of them—no, thousands of them—dancing across every inch of the slatted frames inside the hive box.

"Good morning, my little ladies and gents," said Mage Radix. His voice was soothing, calming. "A beautiful day for you to be out and about. Lots of flowers for your pleasure."

The buzzing of the bees seemed to diminish.

"They can't understand what you're saying, can they?" Wil asked.

"They may not understand my *words*," said Mage Radix. "They have their own ways of speaking or singing, if you will."

Mage Radix lifted one of the frames from the hive and pointed to small chambers filled with glistening honey. "This is where they store their honey," he said, pointing to the outer edge of the frame. "They've capped off the chambers here." Pointing to the middle of the frame, he smiled. "These cells are holding the young, growing bees. A strong, healthy queen will lay her eggs in a spiral pattern. And you can tell the age of the young ones by what colour their eyes are. White eyes are the youngest, then they turn pink and finally purple before turning black—a miracle in three weeks. Ah, such beautiful creatures."

Wil hardly heard what Mage Radix was saying. He stared in fascination at Mage Radix's bare hands, which were completely covered in bees. Mage Radix caressed the bees and still talking in a soft voice, quietly brushed them from his hands and placed the frame back in the hive.

"Lovely day, isn't it?" said a loud voice behind them with no warning.

XIV THE INSPECTOR

Seven of them in a zigzag—the serpentine pattern.

NON CONDUNT APES EXAMINA ANTE TEMPESTATES.
GENERALLY, BEES DO NOT FORM SWARMS BEFORE STORMS.

Mage Radix, Sophie and Wil turned to find an officious-looking man standing there. He was holding a clipboard on which he was scribbling notes. On his head sat an overly large helmet and he was swathed in netting from head to foot; it was hard to see his face.

"May I help you?" asked Mage Radix. His voice sounded suspicious, thought Sophie.

"Yes, Mage Radix, I'm Barton Redelmeier, one of the inspectors-s-s from the Endangered Insects-s-s Division, S.S.M.C.," said the man and he pointed to the photo badge pinned to his shirt.

"I was told the inspectors would make an appointment before coming out here," said Mage Radix, as he peered at the badge through the netting. "The purpose of your visit, Mr. Redelmeier?" he asked.

"I understand you have six hives-s-s, plus the one, Mage Radix," said the inspector, eyeing the beehives. "Six plus-s-s one makes seven." The inspector wrote something on his clipboard. "You've heard, of course, about the new mite that's been identified as a possible culprit in the decimation of the local bee population."

"The new mite?" repeated Mage Radix.

"Yes, the *apiponis-s-s destructor*—it's been identified within the last couple of months or s-s-so. We're working on it, of course, but no breakthroughs yet, unfortunately. Have you noticed anything s-s-strange with your hives-s-s?"

Mage Radix shifted uncomfortably from one foot to the other. "The children are helping me today," he said.

"Yes, of course, Mage Radix, I understand," said the inspector. "Perhaps-s-s we should come back at a more convenient hour. But is there anything you'd like to report in the meantime?" he asked, his pen poised. "Of course, s-s-security measures-s-s have been taken?"

"Of course, Mr. Redelmeier," said Mage Radix, sounding overly polite. "Ah, there was just a small matter."

"S-s-small matter, Mage Radix?"

"A little swarm, Mr. Redelmeier," said Mage Radix. "That's all."

"I see, Mage Radix." said the inspector. "And you know where the new nest is, of course?"

"Well—" said Mage Radix.

"Mage Radix, you do know where the nest is, don't you?" repeated the inspector, his voice hard. "It is of the utmost importance, Mage Radix, that we maintain a precis-s-se inventory. I'm sure you understand. A bee thief is elus-s-sive under the cover of night. Bee-rustling is becoming a big business-s-s. And feral hives are a threat to the whole money, I mean, honey s-s-supply."

"Bees are wild creatures, Mr. Redelmeier, as you must know," said Mage Radix, his voice bristling. "I'm afraid the queen and her colony didn't survive the big storm we had a while back."

"Are you sure you're capable of providing proper supervision for these bees, Mage Radix?"

"Quite sure, Mr. Redelmeier," said Magix Radix coldly.

"Good then," said the inspector in a more cheerful tone. He glanced at Sophie and Wil. "Training the next generation, are we?"

"Yes, this is Rue Isidor's niece Sophie and nephew Wil," said Mage Radix stiffly.

"Oh, Rue Isidor's-s-s little children?" said the inspector, and he adjusted his hat and netting, apparently to get a better look at them. "Interested in bees now, are we? Runs in the family."

Sophie bristled at the word *little* and felt her cheeks flush. Inspector or not, how dare he call me *little*.

She felt Wil's eyes on her. She glanced at him sideways, while still keeping an eye on the inspector. Wil made a round pair of eyeglasses with his thumbs and index fingers, and pointed at her.

Before Sophie could say anything, she felt a sharp pain in her neck. "Ow," she yelped and her eyes watered. "I...I...I think I've been stung."

"What!" exclaimed Mage Radix. "Where?"

Sophie pointed to her neck, which felt all hot and prickly, as if she had just been scorched by a flame.

Mage Radix whipped out a small container of ointment from his pocket, swept Sophie's netting to one side and applied some of the ointment to her neck. The pain subsided immediately.

"A small hole in your netting there, Sophie," said Mage Radix. "That's too bad."

He pulled a small bee from Sophie's netting and whispered to it, "For the good of the whole."

"Well, we'll let you get on with your busines-s-s," said the inspector, and he adjusted his netting, then snapped his clipboard shut. "You'll let us know if there are any fresh developments-s-s, Mage Radix."

"Yes, of course," said Mage Radix, who was still cradling the bee in his hand. From the cold tone of his voice, Sophie was sure Mage Radix would do no such thing.

✦✦✦✦✦✦

"That inspector gave me the creeps," said Sophie, as they walked home.

"I could tell," said Wil. "That's why I was pointing at your glasses. The frames turned fiery red when he called us little."

"I am tired of people calling me little all the time," said Sophie.

"I don't think Mage Radix liked him much either," said Wil. "Why would a bee inspector be completely covered up by netting? You'd think he'd be used to being around bees and getting stung. Mage Radix doesn't wear any special equipment."

"I don't think that instructor actually liked doing his work," said Sophie. "Anyway, wouldn't it be amazing if we could go to the Dragonfly Festival? I'd love to see the man with a bee beard."

"Yeah," said Wil. "But there's no way. Haven't you noticed how worried Aunt Rue looks? I heard her saying that whatever money she's earning at the Secretariat, it's barely enough to feed all of us."

"You're probably right," said Sophie, feeling disappointed.

A small shadow flashed across the sidewalk in front of them. Sophie looked up just in time to see a dragonfly whiz past. She thought for one crazy moment the dragonfly had been listening in on their conversation.

"Did you see that?" she asked.

"What?" said Wil.

"The dragonfly—it flew right over our heads."

"No," said Wil.

"You didn't even see its shadow??"

Wil shook his head. "But then maybe we imagined the green grass too." He pointed to the end of Half Moon Lane as they turned down the street.

Sophie stared. She could not believe her eyes.

The grass had returned to its usual dry, yellow, weedy state. The flowers were gone. And the FOR SALE sign had been taken down, leaving only a gaping hole in the ground.

"I guess nobody wanted to buy the house," she said, her voice flat.

❖❖❖❖❖❖

Wil yawned, pushed aside the pile of books on his bed and slid in under the covers. He had been just as disappointed as Sophie that the house at the end of the block had not been sold. That house will be empty forever, he thought. People must have realized the woman with the dog's tongue suit would say anything to sell it as quickly as possible. People looking at the house would have immediately seen past the green grass and flowers, and realized no one had lived in it for years.

He leaned over to say goodnight to Esme, but she was not hiding in her hut. He looked for her in the earth and his heart began to pound.

"Esme?" he said. "Where are you?" He clawed at the earth.

But Esme was not in her cage.

"Wil, what's wrong?" asked Sophie, standing in the doorway. Her eyes were blurry and unfocused. Wil realized with a start she wasn't wearing her glasses.

"Esme's gone," said Wil in a small voice.

Sophie ran down the hallway. "Aunt Rue! Aunt Violet!" she shrieked.

Aunt Rue's footsteps clattered up the stairs and Aunt Violet, long purple hair in braids and dressing gown trailing, hurried from her room down the hall.

"What happened?" they both asked at the same time, but one look at Wil's stricken face and the open cage was enough.

"Don't worry. Esme can't have gone far," Aunt Rue said. She got down on her hands and knees and began to scour the floor, under Wil's bed, under the dresser, behind the curtains.

If he hadn't felt so sad, Wil would have laughed, for Aunt Rue really did look funny on all fours.

Aunt Violet gave Wil a hug. "I'm sure she'll be all right, Wil. We know she can go a long time without food. She doesn't need to eat every day like us. When she wants to be found, she'll be found."

Wil watched glumly as Sophie stepped over to the window and stared down at the floor.

There was a hole there—a hole Wil had never noticed before. It was small and round—the perfect size, Wil thought.

One tear rolled down his left cheek.

Cadmus sniffed at the empty cage and skulked over to the window beside Sophie; his right paw poked tentatively down the hole.

"What if she doesn't come back? said Wil, his voice trembling. "And will I get in trouble with Mrs. Clop at the S.S.M.C.?"

"Not to worry, Wil," said Aunt Rue. "I'm sure Esme will show up. But I'll take care of alerting Mrs. Clop that she's missing just in case. Children, it's late. Time for little people to be going to bed," said Aunt Rue, as she pulled herself to her feet.

"We're not little," said Sophie, bursting into tears. "Today, that mean bee inspector, his name was Mr. Riddlemeier—called us little; and Minister Skelch called me little before too. It's not fair."

"Calm down, Sophie. I'm sorry. I didn't mean to hurt your feelings," said Aunt Rue, her brow furrowed. She was obviously surprised at Sophie's sudden outburst. "What's all this about a bee inspector?"

"He came to talk to Mage Radix today and asked about one of the bee hives," Wil answered. "He said they had to keep track of the bees."

"Did he say who he was?" asked Aunt Rue.

Why is Aunt Rue asking all these questions about the stupid bee inspector, when Esme is gone? thought Wil.

"He said he was from the Endangered Insects Division," said Sophie, wiping a tear away from her cheek with the back of her hand.

"I don't know anyone named Redelmeier," said Aunt Rue, concern on her face. "There's no one by that name in Endangered Insects—not that I know of."

"Then who was he?" asked Sophie.

"Don't you think the children should get to bed, Rue?" said Aunt Violet quickly, ignoring Sophie's question. "They've had such a busy day."

"You're right, Aunt Violet," said Aunt Rue, catching Aunt Violet's eye. "I don't think there's anything more we can do tonight. I'll check with the Secretariat about it tomorrow."

Aunt Violet ruffled Wil's hair. "We've got a bit of good news for you. Perhaps this will cheer you up." She glanced over at Aunt Rue, whose face lightened a little.

"We have four tickets to the Dragonfly Festival at the end of July," said Aunt Rue.

Sophie wiped her nose on her sleeve. "We just saw the Dragonfly Festival poster today."

Wil tried to smile, but failed miserably.

"It was going to be a surprise," said Aunt Rue. "Minister Skelch wanted to thank you for saving the snakes of Narcisse and helping to capture Rufus Crookshank. And he thought you may appreciate tickets to the festival rather than have some stuffy old ceremony."

XV The Dragonfly Festival

The dragonfly is going to zoom right off
my hand into thin air, thought Sophie.

ULLO NOMINE MEL EST MEL
SED OMNIA MELLA SUNT DISSIMILIA.
HONEY IS HONEY BY ANY OTHER NAME,
ALTHOUGH NOT ALL HONEYS ARE ACTUALLY THE SAME.

Esme had still not been seen or heard from since the day she disappeared from Wil's room two weeks ago. Wil had refused to talk about Esme or even mention her name. But he had also refused to move her cage from by his bed and carefully left an egg on the floor, near the hole.

For some reason, he had also put another egg outside in the backyard near the gargoyle. The egg was always gone the next morning. Privately, Sophie thought a raccoon or skunk probably took it, but Wil seemed to take it as a hopeful sign that Esme was somehow still alive, and was always much cheerier when he saw that it was gone.

The gargoyle, for its part, seemed to think the egg was an offering for Lord Goyle (Sophie's nickname); it no longer glared as ferociously at Wil as it had in the past.

This particular morning, they were both so excited at being able to go to the Dragonfly Festival, that neither of them wanted to eat breakfast. Only after Aunt Rue threatened, "We can't leave until you eat," did they manage a few mouthfuls of toast and jam, and a gulp of orange juice.

⭐⭐⭐⭐⭐⭐

Hundreds of striped tents dotted the field, their colours shimmering in the summer heat.

"Tickets, please," said a young woman sporting a long pair of bobbling antennae.

Aunt Rue handed her the four Dragonfly Festival tickets, and the woman stamped their hands with a purple dragonfly.

The purple dragonfly is going zoom right off my hand, thought Sophie.

"Very nice," said Aunt Violet, as she held her left hand in the air and admired the purple dragonfly. It matched the wobbly purple flower on her sun hat.

Sophie was amused to see several bees were buzzing around the hat and trying to land on top of the flower.

"Here's your festival map," said the young woman with the antennae and she waved them through a towering rainbow archway. A humungous dragonfly carving teetered on top.

"Why don't we go over to the honey tent first—yellow and black stripes," said Aunt Rue, after consulting the map. "Flavia Bottle—an old acquaintance of mine—is running the honey booth this year, and I'd like to say hello."

"Can we see the man with the bee beard?" asked Sophie.

"The man with the bee beard is not too far from the honey tent," said Aunt Rue, peering at the map. "He'll be there at ten o'clock. We'll just have time for a quick visit to the honey tent."

They wended their way past colourful tents selling treasures galore—silk scarves, flashing prisms, wooden flutes, rings and necklaces, hats, shirts, net bags, small glass sculptures, wooden boxes, smelly soaps. Past the jugglers and tall stilt-walkers. Past the popcorn and snow candy stands.

Hundreds of dragonflies swooped and swirled above their heads—it was impossible to count them all. Black and blue,

85

red, golden, iridescent green—Sophie had never known there were so many different kinds.

Flavia Bottle greeted Aunt Rue warmly—a little too warmly, thought Sophie, as though her pleasure were a sham.

"Rue Isidor, how long has it been? What a surprise! Why, the last time I saw you—well, it must be at least ten years ago. You haven't changed one bit."

"Nor you, Flavia," said Aunt Rue. "Strange we've both ended up with a common interest in bees, isn't it?"

"No telling where the winds will carry one," said Flavia Bottle, "is there?"

While Aunt Rue was talking with Flavia Bottle, Sophie, Wil and Aunt Violet inspected the dozens of jars of honey on display.

"Shall we be brave and try some?" asked Aunt Violet.

"As long as we don't try the black one over there," said Sophie, pointing to a jar at the end of the table. She definitely didn't want to try buckwheat honey ever again. "Maybe we'll find that honey with the red streaks in it," she whispered to Wil.

Aunt Rue pulled Sophie and Wil over to the counter. "Flavia, I'd like you to meet my niece Sophie and nephew Wil."

"Hello, children," said Flavia Bottle. "What kind of honey do you like?"

"We saw a different kind of honey at Melilla's," said Wil abruptly.

"Melilla's does have a decent selection," said Flavia Bottle with a sniff, as though she didn't want to mention the name of a competitor.

"It was different than all the other honeys," said Sophie. "It had streaks in it—red streaks."

Flavia Bottle looked startled, then afraid. She seemed to recover herself quickly, however. "Red streaks—that sounds like an unusual honey," she said, clearing her throat. "Perhaps it was a mix of two honeys together. Or sometimes honey changes colour when it gets older. I'm sorry, but I've not heard of that kind before."

Her answer was definite, like a door being shut; it was obvious Flavia Bottle did not want them to ask any more questions.

"That does sound like an unusual kind of honey, Sophie," said Aunt Rue, looking distressed. "Well, lovely seeing you again, Flavia.

Children, let's go see what Aunt Violet is looking at."

Aunt Violet was standing over by a large collection of beeswax candles. "I do love the smell of beeswax," she said. "I wonder if we could get some more wax from Mage Radix."

"Think of how many thousands of hours of work it was for bees to make all this wax," said Aunt Rue.

Sophie was holding a beeswax candle to her nose—the scent was so sweet and intoxicating—when she noticed a woman with pale skin and black hair entering the tent. It was the same woman they had seen at Melilla's and then again with the real estate agent. The woman glided over to the counter and began to talk with Flavia Bottle.

"Pssst, Wil," whispered Sophie, "there she is again," but Wil had obviously already seen her.

"Let's get closer to hear what they're saying," said Sophie.

"We could buy some honey," said Wil.

"Good idea," she whispered.

"Aunt Rue, may we buy a jar?" asked Sophie.

Aunt Rue smiled. "You may each choose one jar," she said. "That will be a great treat."

Wil chose a honey tinged the colour of red amber. HONEYDEW HONEY, the label read—*made by honeybees collecting nectar secreted from another insect, such as an aphid.* "I always thought honey just came from flowers," he said.

"And what would you like, Sophie?" asked Aunt Violet. "There's blueberry here. One of my favourites. It's only after you've tasted it, then you realize it reminds you of a whole field of wild blueberries under a hot, dusty summer sun."

"Why don't you get the blueberry honey, Aunt Violet?" asked Sophie, who thought the blueberry honey looked quite ordinary. "I'd really like to try this greyish one here—EUCALYPTUS HONEY."

"That one will have a strong taste, no doubt," said Aunt Violet. "You wait and see."

Wil and Sophie carried their jars to the counter, which was piled high with a display of new honey samples.

Wil nudged Sophie. "Did you hear what that woman with the black hair said?" he whispered.

"No, what?" asked Sophie.

"I heard her say something about *national security* again," he whispered.

"Children, we'd better hurry," said Aunt Rue. "We don't want to miss the man with the bee beard. The show is—" She stopped short when she saw the woman with the black hair standing at the counter.

"Hello, Rue," said the woman with the black hair, and her eyes flickered over Wil and Sophie.

Aunt Rue smiled, but her smile looked strained, thought Sophie.

Sophie and Wil quickly picked up the two jars of honey from the counter, after Aunt Rue and Aunt Violet had paid for them.

"Who was that woman, Aunt Rue?" asked Sophie, shading her eyes from the bright morning sun, as they all left the tent.

"Deputy Minister Lucretia Daggar," said Aunt Rue. "Works at the Secretariat. She used to be the Senior Assistant and then she got a promotion. So she's high up on the ladder." Aunt Rue sighed. "I should have introduced you, but it would have been awkward. We don't get along particularly well—ever since Cyril…I suppose that's the reason Flavia Bottle was so cool towards me too. Things seem to have gotten worse recently…" Aunt Rue's voice trailed off, and she didn't offer any more information about Lucretia Daggar.

"Lucretia Daggar must have been the Lucie in those photographs," whispered Sophie to Wil.

"Yeah, and I bet she was friends with Rufus Crookshank," whispered Wil.

"Rue, why don't you leave work behind you—just for one day," said Aunt Violet. "Here, smell these beeswax candles. Aren't they sweet?"

Aunt Rue dutifully smelled the candles; but tears came to her eyes.

The candles must remind Aunt Rue of her brother, thought Sophie. Aunt Rue was still lighting a candle every night for her brother. Ten years since my father disappeared…ten years since I was born.

Sophie looked at Wil, and they both looked down, not knowing what to say to comfort Aunt Rue.

XVI Masks

The spiral snakes on his face seemed alive.

UNI VENENUM, ALTERI CIBUS.
POISON FOR ONE, FOOD FOR ANOTHER.

By the time Sophie, Wil, Aunt Violet and Aunt Rue reached the bee beard man, the crowd surrounding him was at least ten people deep.

"Would you believe it?" exclaimed a woman standing in front of Wil.

"What's he doing?" asked Wil, trying to jump up and see what was going on. "I can't see a thing."

"Me neither," said Sophie.

"Children, why don't you slip up to the front there," said Aunt Rue. "Don't push now. We'll wait for you right here."

Sophie and Wil sidled through the crowd, which parted reluctantly, until they were right up front.

Sophie stared up at the man. He was bald and had a long, white beard over which was growing a second beard. Only, the second beard wasn't a beard of hair. It was a mass of buzzing bees!

A bee was crawling up the man's nose, another hung between his eyebrows; a third straggled onto his ear.

"How can he stand it?" she whispered to Wil.

"I don't know," said Wil, "but it's incredible."

The man's eyes gleamed; he smiled at the crowd and waved. "Feels warm and it tickles," he said. "A little like thousands of tiny feathers."

Everyone clapped their hands, the man bowed his head slightly; the bees hummed.

"I think that's the longest bee beard I've ever seen," said Aunt Rue afterwards. "Once I saw man who was wearing a bathing suit, but it was made entirely of bees! I know...I know...not the sort of game I'd want to play either," she said, smiling at Sophie's and Wil's horrified expressions.

"Aunt Violet went to speak with the portrait artist," she said, pointing to a nearby tent with a large sign out front.

A single, large eye was painted on the sign. Vivid blue eye shadow and thick eyeliner curled upwards, framing the eye like the Egyptian eye of Horus. And every once in a while, the eye swivelled, gazed at a passer-by and blinked once...twice.

It was intimidating to be stared at by such a gigantic eye. Sophie tried to imagine how big the person who owned such an eye would be. At least as tall as the MiddleGate Library, she thought.

According to the sign, the artist—Ursula von Scrum, by name—painted portraits of the *Infamous, Famous and Especially Ordinary.*

"Does Aunt Violet want her portrait painted?" asked Sophie, thinking Aunt Violet would probably be in the *Especially Ordinary* category.

"I don't see why she would," said Aunt Rue.

Aunt Violet was talking with a woman who must have been Ursula von Scrum herself, thought Sophie. Even though the tent was filled with lots of portraits, Sophie could not stop staring at her. She had long, long, long red nails, and her painted eyebrows arched over her eyes, down her cheeks and met at her chin. She spoke with a strange accent and her red lips scarcely moved when she spoke; her face was like a still mask.

"So what do you do if a client is not happy with your services?" asked Aunt Violet earnestly.

"No, this is not a problem…not a problem generally," said Ursula von Scrum. She waved her hands in the air and the red nails flashed. "We are vain, of course, as you know; we do love to look at ourselves, do we not, my dear? My art is merely to enhance the innate and unique gifts each and every one of us possesses.

"You do not show a client what they do not want to see. It is for you to lead them to their hopes and dreams. This is the work of artists such as ourselves, my dear."

"What in snake's name are they talking about?" whispered Wil.

"Aunt Violet seems enthusiastic about it, whatever it is," answered Sophie. "She's even taking notes—something about how artists help people understand their dreams."

"How do you decide on your fees?" asked Aunt Violet

"Easier than you may think," said Ursula von Scrum. "How much is the client willing to pay? It's simple, my dear. You offer more—something extra, something special—for those who can pay more. And I do think your idea of referrals, by the way, is a good one. I think we could do something unusual and creative."

"Aunt Rue, what's a referral?" asked Sophie.

"Someone recommends somebody to someone else," said Aunt Rue, who was staring at herself in a round mirror sitting on the table near the tent entrance.

"That sounds confusing," said Sophie.

"Well, suppose you told one of your school friends, *Everyone knows Melilla Morggan makes the best honey candies in the world.* They'd want to meet to go to her shop and try one of her candies, right?" said Aunt Rue, who was still looking at her image in the mirror. She frowned and patted one of her braided coils.

"Right," said Sophie.

"That's what's known as a *referral*," said Aunt Rue. "You're recommending someone's services."

"Are you sure Aunt Violet doesn't want to have a portrait of herself?" asked Sophie, looking around at the paintings hanging in the tent. The eyes of the people all seemed to follow her—it was really creepy having all these eyes staring at you—just like the painting in the house that had been for sale. She wondered if Ursula von Scrum had painted that one too.

Aunt Rue turned away from the mirror and sighed. "Having your portrait done is expensive, children."

✦✦✦✦✦✦

Delicious smells wafted through the air in the Firefly Restaurant tent, making Wil's mouth water. But when they read through the menu, Wil was shocked. Every dish was made from boiled, crushed, baked, fried or roasted insects!

"Why don't we make dinner easy for ourselves and get the *Firefly Special Buffet* with the caterpillar soup, breaded grasshopper, honey-dipped crickets, mushrooms stuffed with maggots, and wild ant pudding with black currants and green mint-aphid sauce," said Aunt Rue, reading from the menu. She smiled. "Doesn't that sound delicious?"

Wil felt like gagging. He wasn't sure which would be worse—a maggot-stuffed mushroom or an ant pudding.

"My dears, people all over the world relish insects," Aunt Violet said. "Rue, what's that word?"

"Entomophagy?" Aunt Rue answered.

"Yes, entomophagy," Aunt Violet repeated, "which means eating insects, has been around for thousands of years—worms, crickets, termites, beetle larvae. Locusts with honey are supposed to be tasty, I've heard. This hors d'œuvre is superb!" she said, biting enthusiastically into a snack of scorpion snaps and green tomato worm paté, while Wil and Sophie watched.

When Wil finally screwed up the courage to try some of the breaded grasshoppers, it was out of sheer desperation because he was so hungry. The grasshoppers were crunchy and nutty in flavour, but tasty, thought Wil, if you could just ignore the bits of leg and antennae sticking up here and there. And the caterpillar soup and honey-dipped locusts were "divine," as Aunt Violet put it. But he could not bring himself to try the maggot-stuffed mushrooms.

He washed down the last bit of ant pudding with a swig of honey spice, which had been served with a dead beetle floating on its back.

Wil had found the beetle so distracting he had quietly removed it and spent the evening trying to ignore its leg, which was peeping out from under his plate.

"As this is your special day—courtesy of Minister Skelch—is there anything else you'd like to do?" asked Aunt Rue.

"Thank you, Aunt Rue and Aunt Violet. This is the best best day we've ever had," declared Wil, and he meant every word.

Aunt Rue smiled, and Wil realized he hadn't seen Aunt Rue really smile in a very long time.

"Can we go to the face-painting tent, Aunt Rue?" asked Sophie.

❖❖❖❖❖❖

"So what will it be?" asked Marco Magnifico, the man who painted faces. Marco Magnifico's own face was covered with spiral designs on his forehead and cheeks that reminded Wil of snakes—one red, the others, orange and yellow. He pointed with a flourish to his tiered trays of powders, paints and pencils. "Any colour your heart desires," he said. "Tell me your mask's wish."

"I…I—" said Sophie, her eyes shining. "I haven't decided yet," she said.

"And you, young sir?" he asked, turning to Wil.

Wil's mind was blank. He felt for the black medallion under his shirt, uncertain what to say. "Um—"

The image of the bee on the black medallion flashed into his mind.

"A bee," he said quietly.

"A bee," repeated Marco Magnifico. "Bees—wise creatures. They sing. They dance. They rob the flowers yet bear them gifts. Loyal to the death. A good choice, young man."

"I've decided," said Sophie suddenly. "A dragonfly!"

"Excellent," said Marco Magnifico. "Ladies first. I will paint the dragonfly and then the bee."

He covered Sophie in a white apron. She looks like she's wrapped in a large cocoon, thought Wil.

"You will sit still, young lady—no wriggling. A dragonfly for your face and a damselfly for one fingernail."

Without her glasses and before Wil's eyes, Sophie's face was not her own. A twelve-spotted skimmer (so named for its spotted wings shimmering blue and black, according to Marco Magnifico) cloaked her cheeks; her nose became the dragonfly's body, a dusky blue.

And a small, perfect damselfly—a river jewelwing, vivid green with neat, folded-back wings tipped black—graced her left thumbnail.

"Dragonflies are magical creatures, the companions of serpents, people say," said Marco Magnifico, his voice dreamy. "Some one hundred different kinds of damselflies and dragonflies have been sighted in these parts." He closed his eyes and began to recite a small poem:

> *Heed the dragonflies.*
> *They hover, they swoop,*
> *they dart, they loop.*
> *Their capacious jaws are wide,*
> *their wings quicksilver.*
> *They will carry you away*
> *o'er field and river,*
> *marsh and lake—*
> *until you shiver,*
> *until you shake.*
> *Heed the great odonata—*
> *the dragon that flies.*

Sophie had a happy, dazed expression in her eyes, as Marco Magnifico held up a mirror to her face.

He turned to Wil. The spiral snakes on his face coiled when he smiled—they seemed to be alive.

Wil was transfixed.

"Your turn, young man," said Marco Magnifico, and he whipped out another white apron.

XVII ΠEW FRIEΠDS

The bee was almost as big as the flower.

EX LASSITUDINE, FACINUS MEMORABILE.
OUT OF BOREDOM, GREAT ADVENTURE.

It was nearing the end of August. Summer vacation was almost over and the hot, sultry, endless days of mid-summer had bowed to cooler nights, cloudy days.

Sophie and Wil were moping about the house. Mage Radix was away until the day after tomorrow so they couldn't visit the beehives; and they were half-heartedly playing a game of circular serpent's chess. Neither of them had made a move in the last quarter hour.

Aunt Violet was busy in the kitchen, harvesting her herbs, bundling them up and hanging them in her drying cupboard.

And Aunt Rue had gone to England for the beekeeping conference. She wouldn't be back for at least another week; and had sent them a postcard with a picture of a bee and a dragonspot lily—the bee was almost as big as the flower.

There is more honey here than at the Dragonfly Festival and Melilla's. I've tried wild thyme honey from Greece, orange blossom honey from

the U.S., lavender honey from France. Our buckwheat honey has
been a great hit. I went to a really interesting presentation about
poisonous honeys. Miss you all. Love, Aunt Rue

How could honey be poisonous? thought Sophie. She sighed as she looked at the chip of green polish on her thumbnail—all that remained of the damselfly painted by Marco Magnifico. It was as though the Dragonfly Festival had never happened, she mused, as she gazed out the window at a fat worm suspended on a filament. Blowing in the breeze, it tugged upwards and clutched a small wad of silk about which it spiralled and danced. It reminded Sophie of Esme rolling one of her eggs. She sighed again.

After the Dragonfly Festival, all leads about why the honeybees were sick had completely fizzled. Perhaps she and Wil had imagined the whole thing—made a mountain out of a molehill, an ostrich egg out of a quail egg, a lake out of a puddle...

"Your move," said Wil, startling Sophie from her reverie.

"But I thought it was your move," said Sophie.

"I've been waiting for you for at least fifteen minutes!" exclaimed Wil, looking annoyed.

Before they could argue any further, there was the sound of commotion outside. It was a moving truck rumbling down the street—a truck so large that it took up practically the entire width of Half Moon Lane. On the side of the van were large letters painted colours of the rainbow:

OVER THE RAINBOW MOVING COMPANY *(since 1899)*
Don't Make a Move Without Us

"Do you think someone actually bought the house?" asked Sophie excitedly.

"Let's go see," said Wil.

Happily abandoning their game of serpent's chess, they ran out the door and trotted down the sidewalk.

The truck had indeed pulled up right in front of the house at the end of Half Moon Lane. By the time they reached the house, the movers were already starting to carry boxes inside.

Wil and Sophie crept around to the side of the house, as they had before, and peered in the window. The house looked bright and cheerful. Gone were the dusty, old stuffed furniture and dour portraits. The mantel was already filled with framed photographs and the mirror above was so shiny Wil and Sophie could see a reflection of themselves peering in the window. Boxes were being trotted up the stairs and Sophie saw a woman standing at the base of the stairs with a checklist.

"It's Mrs. Bain, the woman who asked if someone had died in the house," she said excitedly.

"I can't believe it," said Wil.

"Who are you?" said a voice behind them.

They turned around. A boy and a girl about the same height as Wil and Sophie were staring curiously at them. Both had round faces covered with freckles and the greenest eyes Sophie had ever seen.

"I'm Sophie, and this is my cousin Wil," said Sophie.

"Who are you?" asked Wil.

"I'm Beatriz," said the girl.

"And I'm Phinneas," said the boy. "We're twins. You want to see our new house?"

Sophie and Wil followed Beatriz and Phinneas up the steps and into the house. Sophie was surprised to see the floor had black and white tiles. She had remembered a dirty, shaggy, brown carpet. There was a long, gleaming table in the dining room.

"Your house is really different," said Sophie.

"It feels happy," said Wil emphatically.

"It's empty though," said Phinneas. "We're the only ones here right now. We came to help Mum. Elenie and Oliver and Luther are coming with Dad next week. They're the oldest."

"And Ziggy—don't forget Ziggy," said Beatriz. "He's the youngest."

"Ziggy has a pet rat named Alfred," said Phinneas. "Alfred and Ziggy are staying with our grandparents for a few days."

Mrs. Bain came in from the kitchen and smiled broadly. "Some new friends, children? Oh, you're the two children we met the first day we saw the house, aren't you?"

"We hoped you'd buy the house," said Sophie. "But then the FOR SALE sign disappeared."

"We thought the woman in the dog's...I mean, in the pink suit couldn't sell it."

"We loved the house from the very first day we saw it," said Mrs. Bain, laughing. "And her suit really was the colour of a dog's tongue, wasn't it?" she said.

"How did you know I was thinking..." Wil's voice trailed off, and he looked guilty.

The suit *had* been the colour of a dog's tongue, thought Sophie—although it was a little uncanny how Mrs. Bain knew exactly what Wil had been thinking.

"Excuse me, kids," said one of the movers, who was carrying a large box labelled FRAGILE.

"Children, careful or you'll be squashed flat by one of these boxes!" said Mrs. Bain. She crossed off another item from her checklist.

"I have an idea if you don't want to get squashed flat," said Sophie, surprised at how quickly she had felt that Beatriz and Phinneas were going to be their friends forever. "Beatriz and Phinneas, you can come with us the day after tomorrow—and meet Mage Radix—he's our botanicals teacher and the beekeeper at Gruffud's. We've been helping him all summer. We'll take a picnic with us—it's our birthday."

Beatriz and Phinneas looked extremely pleased. "You have the same birthday? Are you twins too?"

"No, we're cousins," said Sophie. "But our birthdays are both on August 21st."

XVIII Revoltin' Developments

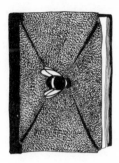

It takes twelve honeybees their entire lifetimes to make one teaspoon of honey.

MODO NUNTIUS BONUS EST
MODO NUNTIUS MALUS
DEINDE ET BONUS ET MALUS,
ERGO CONTUNDAS MUSCAM NUMQUAM
SUPER CRUSTUM VACCINIUM
QUOD CRUSTUM EMICABIT IN OCULUM TUUM.
SOMETIMES THE NEWS IS GOOD AND
SOMETIMES THE NEWS IS BAD, BUT
SOMETIMES THE NEWS IS GOOD AND BAD,
SO NEVER SWAT A FLY ON A BLUEBERRY PIE
OR THE BLUEBERRY PIE WILL SQUIRT IN YOUR EYE.

A large, heavy box arrived the next morning at 9 Half Moon Lane from Mr. Bertram. A letter to *William Wychwood* was glued to the outside. Wil tore it open immediately.

Harbinger Street, Toronto   *August 20th*

Dear Wil:

You will be happy to know I have taken your advice (and Sophie's). The Board Members of the MiddleGate Library Society have offered me a position as the MiddleGate Librarian.

I accepted the offer today.

Of course, there are lots of books here to sort through, but I hope to move sometime in early autumn.

I am sending you a book about bees (aptly named 'The Bee Book'), which I found hiding inside another book. I thought you may find it useful.

I am also sending some other books for you and Sophie to read, as I know the MiddleGate Library has been closed since Rufus Crookshank was arrested.

Please be careful. The Snake in the Grass is not one to give up easily.

Yours sincerely,

Bartholomew Bertram

"Mr. Bertram is coming to MiddleGate!" exclaimed Wil. "He's going to be the librarian."

Aunt Violet, who was just coming into the kitchen for breakfast, yawned and said in a sleepy voice, "I staying up too late last night reading. What did I miss?"

"Mr. Bertram's coming to MiddleGate," said Sophie excitedly. "He's coming to live here."

"Well, it's about time," said Aunt Violet. "I've been telling him that for years. The tea leaves hinted he'd make a decision soon."

"You've been telling him for years?" asked Wil.

"It wasn't right he felt he had to leave MiddleGate after Cyril disappeared," said Aunt Violet. "Mind you, I don't fault him. It's not been an easy ten years. And…of course, Rue and all…didn't make it any easier."

"What's Aunt Rue got to do with Mr. Bertram leaving Middle Gate?" asked Sophie, her eyes bright. Her eyeglass frames turned bright pink.

"Nothing but ancient history," said Aunt Violet hastily. "Nothing at all."

"Does Aunt Rue know Mr. Bertram is coming?" asked Wil.

"I don't suppose so. Aren't you going to look in the box?" said Aunt Violet, changing the subject.

When they opened the box, a small book fell out on the floor—*The Bee Book*. Wil leafed through it quickly. It was filled with advice about how to take proper care of bees and had lots of honey recipes at the back.

His eyes caught a sentence or two.

Bee-bread, a mixture of honey and pollen (known as 'ambrosia' in Greek myth), is surely a food fit for the gods, if there were such beings—liquid gold.

Iamus, the ancestor of a famous family of seers at Olympia was the son of Apollo and Evadne. He was abandoned by his mother and fed honey by two serpents.

Some believe honey is a catalyst for transfiguration and prophecy. Others merely like to spread honey on their morning toast, blissfully unaware that it takes twelve honeybees their entire lifetimes to make one teaspoon of honey. Most honeys are delicious and sweet but there are some honeys that are highly poisonous to humans.

And when he leafed to page 99, his heart jumped, for he recognized the photograph immediately.

"What's that?" asked Sophie, looking over his shoulder. "I wouldn't want to meet that on the stairs."

"Remember the night that man sold you the crystal ball, Aunt Violet?" asked Wil. "And we were looking at the crystal ball, the *Princess* one?" He hesitated, then blurted out, "I saw something."

"Yes," said Aunt Violet slowly, "but you would only have seen a reflection of yourself. Not just anybody can look into a crystal ball and see something—not without the proper training and study."

"I saw a face," said Wil, "but it wasn't my face. It was something else."

"What?" asked both Sophie and Aunt Violet.

"That," said Wil, pointing at the picture of what was a bee's greatly magnified head, according to the caption underneath. "It was a horrible, hairy face…with five eyes—two bulging eyes and three small ones in the middle of its head…and the face was staring right at me."

"That's why you looked so scared," said Sophie. "I thought you were afraid you'd cracked the crystal ball."

"What does that mean if I saw a bee's head in the crystal ball, Aunt Violet?" asked Wil.

I think it means you're letting your imagination run away with you," said Aunt Violet, smiling, but Wil detected a shadow of concern in her eyes.

"And where do we get an imagination from?" asked Sophie mischievously.

"Don't be impertinent, Sophie," said Aunt Violet, but she smiled as she slathered extra black currant jelly on Sophie's and Wil's toast.

XIX SWALLOWED

"Why don't you have your picnic in the small
greenhouse at the back?" said Mage Radix.

VERBORUM CAVE MULSUM SONUM;
VERBA SICUT APES PUNGANT.
BEWARE THE HONEYED SOUND OF WORDS;
LIKE BEES, THEY CAN STING.

Wil and Sophie woke up so early on their birthday that Cadmus refused to open more than one sleepy eye. He stretched once then continued to snooze curled up in a ball on the sofa, while they clattered around in the kitchen.

Wil carefully wrapped up four chocolate chip cookies and packed them in the picnic basket. "What if Beatriz and Phinneas don't come?" he asked.

"Didn't you see how excited they were?" said Sophie. "I think we're going to be friends."

"But maybe they've changed their minds," he said.

Sophie gave him a withering look, and pulled out a jar of dill pickles to take with them. "You can boil some water so we can have hard-boiled eggs. You can't have a picnic without hard-boiled eggs," she said emphatically.

Never having been on a picnic before, Wil dared not argue, even if the eggs did remind him of Esme. He felt a lump in his throat...well, there was no point in thinking about Esme now—not when they had new friends.

They had almost finished packing the picnic when Aunt Violet entered the kitchen. She was still wearing her dressing gown, and her hair was in such a tangle she must have spent the entire night tossing and turning in her bed.

"Were you reading late again, Aunt Violet?" asked Wil.

"Those books you found have been so useful, children," said Aunt Violet. "I really should get a little more sleep, I think…but I have so many ideas in my head."

"What kind of ideas?" asked Sophie.

"Good ideas," said Aunt Violet briskly. "Now, I think we've still got a fresh bottle of honey from the Dragonfly Festival. It's not been opened," said Aunt Violet. "Why don't you take it with you?" She popped a small jar of honey in the picnic basket.

Beatriz and Phinneas knocked on the door just as the grandfather's clock began to chime ten bells.

"Make sure you're home by mid-afternoon. I need some help with the dried herbs," said Aunt Violet, as Sophie and Wil skipped out the front door. "And children—"

Sophie and Wil both turned.

"Happy Birthday, dears," she said, and blew them both a kiss with her two hands.

✦✦✦✦✦

"Ah, the bees knew they were going to have special visitors today," said Mage Radix. "Just moved to MiddleGate have you, Beatriz and Phinneas, was it? Guess you're going to be coming to Gruffud's for school.

"I've got a few chores to do—couple of fence posts to dig in. Why don't you have your birthday picnic in the small greenhouse at the back—the windows are open so it's nice and cool there for you. We'll see if we can find some extra bee suits for you, and you can help me gather a snatch of honey today.

"Lots of dragonflies out. A regular dragonfly convention. It's like the Dragonfly Festival here."

✦✦✦✦✦✦

It was a perfect day for a picnic. The sky was clear and cool, and Mage Radix was right. The dragonflies were out by the hundreds, swooping through the fields and over the greenhouse, their wings glistening in the sunlight like rainbow prisms.

"I hated our last school," said Beatriz, as they sat down on four old boxes in the greenhouse. "We were the only mage family there. It was great news when Mum found out she got this new job."

"Where is she working?" asked Wil.

"She's setting up a new clinic at the MiddleGate Sanatorium, the one for magical maladies."

"I remember she said there was at least one ghost or something in your new house," said Sophie.

"Yeah, she's still working on that," said Phinneas. "It's not been cooperating. Keeps make bumping noises and opening doors at night."

"What's your dad do?" asked Wil.

"He's writing a book about some famous architect. He burned the soup last night, because he totally forgot about it. He's really absent-minded sometimes."

"We live with our Aunt Rue and Aunt Violet," said Sophie. "Wil just moved to MiddleGate last autumn, after his grandmother died. And my parents disappeared just after I was born."

"That must be hard, not having any parents," said Beatriz, with pity in her voice.

"It's okay. Aunt Violet and Aunt Rue take really good care of us," said Sophie. "And I have a cat named Cadmus and Wil has a snake—" Sophie stopped, when she saw the look on Wil's face.

"You have a snake?" said Phinneas.

"Well, I did have one," said Wil, "but she disappeared a month ago. She'll come back soon."

An awkward silence hung in the air.

Sophie desperately tried to think of something to say. "Esme is a really great snake. She saved Wil and me from being kidnapped by a man named Rufus Crookshank."

"Hey, we read about you in the newspaper," said Phinneas, looking impressed.

"And you saved the snakes of Narcisse from being murdered, didn't you?" said Beatriz.

"Is there really a Serpent's Chain?" asked Phinneas eagerly.

"Yes," said Wil. "And we've found out something else."

Phinneas and Beatriz leaned forward.

"It's about some bees here," said Sophie. "And they're not ordinary bees; they're magical bees and they've been getting sick."

"No one knows why," said Wil.

"It could be something called an *apiponis destructor*, which is a bee mite, a parasite—it lives on the bees," said Sophie. "A woman named Lucretia Daggar is involved somehow. She works high up in the Secretariat on the Status of Magical Creatures—actually, it turns out she's the one you bought your house from. We found some old photos down by the river at your place. And the names Lucie and Rufus were on the back of them. So Lucretia Daggar—Lucie—must have been friends with Rufus Crookshank when they were young. And we found out something else too."

"What?" asked Phinneas and Beatriz, wide-eyed.

"Did you know that some honey is poisonous?" said Sophie.

"How can honey be poisonous?" asked Beatriz.

"Honey made from the flowers of the horsechestnut tree is poisonous," said Sophie. "Mage Radix told us."

"Yes, but it's poisonous to humans, not the bees," Wil pointed out.

"Well, what if something is poisoning the bees?" said Beatriz.

"Speaking of poison, who wants to drink the pickle juice?" asked Phinneas with a grin.

"You're kidding," said Wil with a grimace. "That's way too sour."

"Want to make a bet?" said Phinneas, and he picked up the jar of pickle juice and took a swig.

Not to be outdone, Wil took the jar himself. The smell of the pickle juice made his eyes water, but he closed his eyes and swallowed.

The pickle juice was so sour he coughed and spluttered. Phinneas patted him on the back. "Wasn't so bad, was it?"

"Delicious," said Wil, grimacing as he wiped his mouth with his sleeve.

"Look, forgot about the honey," said Sophie and she pulled out the small jar. "What kind is this? Do you remember, Wil?"

"Aunt Violet said it was one we got at the Dragonfly Festival," said Wil.

"It must be the eucalyptus honey, but I thought it was more greyish," said Sophie, shaking the bottle a little. She opened the jar and peered into it.

"It must change colour when it's older," said Wil. "Remember Flavia Bottle said honey changes colour sometimes?"

"It smells good," said Sophie, and she took a spoonful of honey and drizzled some on a crust of fresh bread.

"Wait," said Wil. "Let's pretend this is magic honey. It gives you the power to tell the future, but only if you know the secret words."

"What are the secret words?" asked Phinneas.

Wil thought for a moment. "I know," he said, and he pulled out his notebook. "Where are they?" He flipped through a few more pages.

"What are you looking for?' asked Sophie.

"The names of those honeys from New Zealand," said Wil. "I wrote them down when we were in Melilla's Honey Shop." He flipped through a few more pages of the notebook. "Here they are—*tawari, kamahi, manuka, pohutukawa.* There are four names and four of us...perfect."

"*Tawari, kamahi, manuka—*" repeated Sophie, Beatriz and Phinneas.

"What was that last one?" asked Beatriz.

"*Pohutukawa,*" said Wil.

"*Tawari, kamahi, manuka, pohutukawa,*" they all chanted.

"That sounded really good," said Wil with a grin.

"All right, Wil and I will go first," said Sophie, breaking the bread into two pieces. "We'll close our eyes, and take a bite of the bread and honey at the same moment; and Phinneas and Beatriz, you'll close your eyes and say the secret chant."

Wil and Sophie each took a bite of the bread.

Beatriz and Phinneas covered their eyes with hands and chanted, "*Tawari, kamahi, manuka, pohutukawa.*"

Outside, dragonfly wings flashed past and hundreds of tiny rainbows filled the greenhouse.

XX Abuzz

APIS ALIAM APEM NOSCIT.
ONE BEE KNOWS ANOTHER

XXI Vanished

There was the eerie sound of silence in the greenhouse.

NIL NISI LUDUS FUIT.
BUT IT WAS JUST A GAME.

There was the eerie sound of silence in the greenhouse—but for the zing of the dragonflies flying past outside, a couple of bees buzzing around the honey spoon and one cricket chirping from some hidden place.

"Can we open our eyes yet?" asked Beatriz.

There was no answer.

Phinneas opened his eyes. "Bea, they're gone!" he exclaimed.

Beatriz blinked in the bright sunlight. "Gone? Gone where?"

"How should I know?" said Phinneas. "My eyes were covered!"

"Well, so were mine," said Beatriz, gazing around the greenhouse. "They must be hiding somewhere."

They searched behind the boxes in the corner of the greenhouse. Nothing, but three fat wolf spiders.

"There isn't anywhere else to hide, is there?" said Phinneas. "And I didn't hear the greenhouse door open. So where are they?"

"It must be the secret spell," said Beatriz.

"But it was just pretend," said Phinneas.

Beatriz tugged at the greenhouse door. "We've got to get Mage Radix."

They hurried from the small greenhouse across the field to the beehives, where Mage Radix was hammering in a new fencepost. As they ran, they waved their hands and yelled, "Mage Radix!"

"Better not come too close, children. You're not wearing your bee suits yet," he replied and continued his hammering. "I'll be finished up in a snake's jiffy."

"Mage Radix, something terrible has happened," shouted Beatriz and she pointed to back to the small greenhouse.

Mage Radix stopped hammering. "What's that you said?"

"They're gone," shouted Phinneas.

"What's gone?"

"Sophie and Wil—they've DISAPPEARED!" Phinneas and Beatriz shouted together.

"Disappeared?" Still carrying his large sledge hammer, Mage Radix strode across the field to Beatriz and Phinneas.

"They were there," said Phinneas, "then…all of a sudden—"

"—they weren't," said Beatriz. "They vanished."

"Into thin air," said Phinneas.

"You're sure they're not hiding somewhere?" said Mage Radix with a smile.

"Wepretendedwehadmagichoneyandwemadeupasecretspell," said Beatriz so quickly she didn't stop to take even one breath.

"Sowecouldpredictthefutureandweclosedoureyesandthenthey weregonenotoureyesSophieandWiltheyweregone." Phinneas's face turned red with the effort of telling Mage Radix all this.

"Calm down, children," said Mage Radix. "I can barely understand you. So, you were saying some special words, and then what happened?'

"Wil and Sophie were eating some bread and honey," said Phinneas, slowing down his words with great effort. "They had their eyes closed, and we had our eyes closed, and we said the magic words Wil had in his notebook, and then, they just, just disappeared."

Mage Radix, without another word, threw down the sledge hammer, hurried back to the small greenhouse and yanked the door open. There, on the table was Wil's notebook open to the words *tawari, kamahi, manuka* and *pohutukawa*.

"Those are the names of honeys from New Zealand," said Mage Radix.

"Wil told us he wrote those down when he was at Melilla's Honey Shop," said Beatriz.

Both the children were crying now.

"It was just a game," whimpered Beatriz.

"I don't know what's going on," said Mage Radix, his face grim. He closed the greenhouse windows. "We have to let the school principal and the Secretariat know what's happened. And we'll leave everything just as it is. I'll get you home safely, and after that—" He sighed. "—and after that, I'll go speak to the Isidors."

Beatriz bent down to pick up the picnic basket.

"Just leave it," said Mage Radix gently. "There could be an important sign here, and we just don't see it."

XXII Sweet

He flew into the Air, relishing the Pull of Sunlight on his
Wings, then landed on the Branch of the Tree.

DICIS, PRECOR, LINGUAM APEM?
OMNIBUS UNUS, OMNES UNI.
UNUS MULTIS, UNUS TOTI.
NOS UNUM, UNUM NOS.
PARDON ME. DO YOU SPEAK BEE?
ONE FOR ALL, AND ALL FOR ONE.
ONE FOR THE MANY, ONE FOR THE SUM.
WE ARE ONE, AND WE ARE ONE.

A small Bee with a thick Black and Gold Patch of Fur gleaming on his Belly was standing on a great Plain, pitted with Craters and Seed Boulders. The scent of sticky, intoxicating *Sweet* poured into his Bee-Brain. Every bit of his Fur tingled with Pleasure at the Thought of *Sweet*. Filled up with his new Senses—the World had become a Kaleidoscope of Colours and Smells—several Bee-Moments passed before he realized that he (known as Wil in human-tongue) had become a Bee. How this had happened he did not know, nor could he ask.

As Wil stretched his Legs—all six of them—then carefully cleaned his two Antennae with his Forefeet, he became conscious of a soft, droning Chant in his Head. It was a comforting, humming Noise, or perhaps it was a Smell or a Taste; he couldn't tell which. The hypnotic, rhythmic Chant throbbed

One for All and All for One.
One for the Many, One for the Sum.
April, May, June, July,
There's Work to be Done,
Work to be Done.
Left, Right, Up-down-around,
Sweet, Sweet, Sweet
Work to be Done.
Left, Right, Up-down-around,
Sweet, Sweet, Sweet.
Moon, Sun, Wind and Rain,
Left, Right, Up-down-around,
Sweet, Sweet, Sweet.

No sooner did the Chant end, than it began again, like an endless Loop of tangled Dandelions.

Another Bee landed beside him on the great Plain. She had white Bee-Fur on the top of her Head above large prism Eyes. *Sweet,* she buzzed quickly as a form of Greeting, and the white Fur turned pink.

Sophie, he thought, you're a Bee too—only Sophie in Bee-Tongue translated roughly as *She-Sister-We-Share.* Wil buzzed his four Wings in excitement and tried to speak, but couldn't summon the human Words. All that came out was a low Buzz of Greeting. *S-w-e-e-e-e-t.*

Sophie flew off in a slow Circle around him, did several Loops, landed back down beside him and began to preen her Antennae, as though she had been a Flier her whole Life.

He stretched his Wings and tried fanning them, but it was hard Work, and he was soon quite out of Breath.

She buzzed and danced around him; her Buzz turned into a Laugh (*Fur-Tickle* in Bee-Tongue), and she turned around to show him her Stinger, which had vicious Barbs.

Wil backed off; he didn't have a Stinger. *Dangerous,* he buzzed. *Don't wave that in my Face.*

Sophie buzzed loudly, obviously pleased with her new Body.

Remember you die if you use that thing, buzzed Wil.

Sophie turned her Back on him and began to groom her Antennae.

Another Message began to loop around in Wil's Head, a Message which he did not completely understand. He wondered if Sophie could hear the same Message.

She, the Mother-of-Us-All,
She, the Shining Sun,
Bids Us Build, Bids Us Build,
For Winter Will Come, Winter Will Come.
We are One, and We are One.

The Message had a threatening Quality to it—it made him anxious. Wings abuzz, he pushed off like some awkward black Beetle and flew in a Circle over Sophie's Head. Very pleased with himself, he landed—but it was with a Splat on a large Lake of golden Liquid, which smelled like a Field of Pink Clover—make that ten Fields of Pink Clover.

Sweet, he thought, as he picked himself up and began to clean his Feet and Antennae.

Sophie buzzed noisily and he caught the Meaning. Home (*Place of Twinkling Darkness* in Bee-Tongue), her Buzzing said.

Home, Home, Fly Away Home
Our Dwelling is on Fire
and Our Queen Is Alone.

With a final shake of his second left Leg, he flexed his Wings and followed her high above the Lake of *Sweet.*

The Sunlight tickled and teased them—fruitlessly, the two Bees buzzed against the Clear, searching for a way to the Outside as the Sun began its Descent.

A great armoured Creature with ferocious Jaws zoomed past and Wil jumped back from the Clear in Fright and darted to the Ceiling. His eyes caught sight of a dark Hole. *Out,* he thought, and he zipped into the Hole; Sophie, as quick as he, followed scarcely a Bee-Breath behind.

Together, they crept out into the waning Sunlight, savouring the clean Smell of darkening Bee-Purple Sky. The Message inside his Head changed suddenly.

We Shall Defend the Mother-of-Us-All,
We shall Defend Her, the Shining Sun, the Silvered Moon,
She Bids Us Be Ready, Be Ready, Be Ready
For They Will Come, They Will Come.
We are One, and We are One.

Ignoring the sense of Threat in the Message, he flew high into Air to catch up with Sophie, relishing the Pull of the last Rays of Sunlight on his Wings. He landed on the Branch of a Tree and watched as Sophie spiralled higher and looped twice across the great Green below—but it wasn't just any Green.

Only much later would he be able to express what *Green* meant in Bee-Tongue. It meant a thousand fractals of Blues, Blacks, Whites and Yellows amidst Greens. It meant the Sounds and Smells of Colours calling to him—the Wingstrokes of Violet Blue, low Hums of Siren Song and Fragrances both light and mischievous. The Flowers twinkled, calling to him like Stars in the Night Sky call to humans—the flapping Yellows strident, clamouring, selfish and irresistible, Colours to swallow you up; the Licks of White, their Petals as luminous as young Bees in the Nursery. And holding them all, the Green—not just one Green…but hundreds of Greens. Greens that groan, mumble, shout, hold you, whisper and won't let you go, unless you promise to gaze into them forever. With his five Eyes—for he had not only two large Eyes each with thousands of Lenses, but also three single Eyes in the Middle of his Forehead—he could see Things that no human would ever see…the round Eyes beckoning from the deep Yellow Black-Eyed Susan Daisies, Patterns invisible to human Eyes.

He was so caught by the Sound of the Colours, ever shifting as the Sun set, that he failed to notice a great winged Monster—its Beak, huge, toothless, gaping.

(A sparrow, he would realize later. A common creature, which chirped, hopped here and there in search of he knew not what. A harmless creature, he had always thought. He would never think of sparrows in the same way again.)

With a frightened Buzz that telegraphed *Follow me to Baskets-of-Sweet* (flowers in human-tongue), he zoomed in a dead feint to Ground and dove into the nearest Flowers he could find—Dragonspot Lilies, Purple-Violet Flowers with Black Spot Moles. Trembling and blanketed in intoxicating Pollen, it was a long Time before he peered out from his Hidey-Hole.

The head of the nearest Dragonspot Lily was bowing almost to the Ground. *Sophie hiding,* he thought.

The horrible winged Monster, swooped close by, looped thrice in the Air, then dove and swirled high again, as if chasing Something.

Whatever it was chasing must have flown towards the Shining Comb (greenhouse in human-tongue), for the Monster took off in that Direction.

Wil emerged from his Dragonspot Lily and buzzed, *Sweet?*

No familiar Buzz answered his own.

Instead, a huge, round Hairybee several times his own Size emerged from the Dragonspot Lily and buzzed angrily. *Buzz out. Mine.*

Wil's four Wings sagged and a dreadful Sensation seeped into his Bee-Gut.

That Monster with the Beak had been chasing Something and what if the Something had been Sophie?

Without a backward Glance at the Hairybee, he took off into the Air and headed straight to the Shining Comb—now a brilliant Orange in the Light of the Down-Sun—making sure to fly low in case the Monster returned.

He circled around the Shining Comb, hoping to see Sophie. But after several Circles and no Sightings, he landed on top of a warm Stone on the Roof of Big CombStone (known as Gruffud's Academy in human-tongue).

As he sunned himself, the Chant inside his Head changed again. *Ho-o-o-o-o-me. Ho-o-o-o-o-me. Ho-o-o-o-o-me...* Thousands of Bees were all humming on the same delicious note of *Sweet.*

Following the Sound—or was it the Smell or Taste?—of *Hummmmm,* he crawled to the edge of the warm Stone. Dozens of Bees were coming straight at the Stone. Some swerved and dipped, others flew in a great, long S. And there were other Bees flying away fast and hard...in unerring Bee-Lines.

The *Hummmmm* seemed to be coming from somewhere deep inside the Stone. Entranced, he peered under the Stone.

There was Sophie! All in one furry Piece and covered in Dragonspot Lily Pollen.

Her Wings fanned, *Buzzzzz,* as in *What took you so long?*

Sweet, he replied. *What about the Beaked Monster?*

No big deal, she buzzed. Her Antennae pointed to a Black Cave carved into the Stone. *Great Nest.*

❖❖❖❖❖❖

As the sun set, would anyone looking up have noticed two small honeybees crawling into the mouth of the gargoyle atop Gruffud's Academy for the Magical Arts?

❖❖❖❖❖❖

Far below, Mage Radix frowned at the bee inspector, bedecked in his thick veil of netting as before.

"You're back again, Mr. Redelmeier," asked Mage Radix, his voice cold. "I checked with the Secretariat and they had no record of your name. Who are you and what are you doing here?"

"There must be s-s-some mistake, my dear man," said the inspector, his clipboard poised. He looked up towards the sky and made a quick note. "I'll ensure their records get updated. You know government agencies—they can hardly keep track of their own finances-s-s half the time, and with more s-s-scandals percolating below the s-s-surface than there are s-s-snakes at Narcisse, well, you know..." He laughed, but stopped and cleared his throat when Mage Radix did not join in.

Mage Radix's eyes narrowed, "As far as I'm concerned, you're trespassing on Gruffud's Academy grounds, and I'm asking you

118

to leave. We've had enough goings-on here today with the two children disappearing."

"Oh?" said the inspector. "How distressing."

"Yes, Rue Isidor's little niece and her nephew too," said Mage Radix.

"Yes, of course. Thank you for your cooperation to-date, Mage Radix," said the inspector in an oily, ingratiating way. "We've got all the information we need."

"And what information would that be?" Mage Radix asked coldly, his voice bristling as much as a porcupine clenches its quills.

"The bees are obviously healthy—all eight hives," said the inspector enthusiastically, snapping his clipboard shut. "Seems like it's been a good s-s-summer for you," said the inspector, and his gaze strayed skyward for a moment.

It wasn't until after the inspector left that Mage Radix realized the man had said eight instead of seven. Completely incompetent and a fraud, thought Mage Radix, when there were clearly seven hives in plain sight. That shifty-eyed fellow snooping about made him nervous.

He walked to the beehive with the red stripe and placed his hand on it. The bees from the hive zinged past Mage Radix, intent on their last foray to the wildflowers beyond Gruffud's West Field.

Apis mellifera magykalis—what was so special about these bees? He'd never heard of them before this summer. The Secretariat hadn't told him much—only that they were wild bees and did not domesticate easily...and would he mind taking care of just one hive for the summer?

"Cautionary, protective measures, Mage Agassiz and Mage Radix," Minister Skelch had said in a meeting in the principal's office. "We greatly appreciate your discretion about this matter. No need to mention to anyone this hive is on the property. The *magykalis* hives are all being dispersed for security reasons. You understand, I'm sure, we are not at liberty to disclose complete information about such security matters."

Mage Agassiz had bowed her head. "As Principal of Gruffud's Academy, I'll speak for both Mage Radix and myself; we're pleased to be able to assist, of course, Minister Skelch."

That was all he had been told, and if they swarmed, he was to advise the Secretariat about the new hive's whereabouts. But as far as he knew, there hadn't been any swarms, not since that last queen and her swarm had perished.

But that shifty-eyed fellow had been looking for something. And why had he been looking up at the sky?

Too dark to see anything much...I'll take a look in the morning. He shook his head. Rain coming in tonight; I can feel it in my bones, he thought to himself.

By Draco, he hoped that Sophie Isidor and Wil Wychwood were safe. Surely the Firecatchers would find them soon. Surely, they couldn't have gone far.

XXIII Classified Information

Every time the dragonflies flashed by, there were
dozens of rainbows in the greenhouse.

TEMPUS, TEMPUS, TEMPUS, TEMPUS—
TEMPUS VERBIS TEMPUS FACTIS
TEMPUS SOMNO TEMPUS SOMNIIS
TEMPUS, TEMPUS, TEMPUS, TEMPUS FUGIT!
TIME, TIME, TIME, TIME—
A TIME FOR WORDS, A TIME FOR DEEDS,
A TIME FOR SLEEP, A TIME FOR DREAMS.
TIME, TIME, TIME, TIME FLEES.

Birthday presents sat unopened on the living room table. A large
birthday cake in the shape of a dragonfly sat untouched on the
kitchen table. With every tick of the grandfather's clock, the brightly
coloured balloons hanging from the ceiling seemed to lose more air
and their sagging skin wizened. It was ten o'clock at night, the air
felt mouldy and damp from rain, and there had been no word from
the Firecatchers.

Aunt Violet dunked a sachet of herbs into her crackled, yellow
teapot. Her nose wrinkled as the air filled with the smell of freshly
mown grass, lavender waving in a summer breeze and a dash of
bracing mint.

"That ought to do it—a good, stimulating dose," she said. "One part dried mugwort, one part dried lavender flowers, spearmint and a pinch of chamomile, rose petals and dried rosemary."

"What kind of tea is that?" asked Aunt Rue.

"It's *Dreamnought Tea*. Perhaps a dream will lead us to the children, since the Firecatchers and the Secretariat seem at such a loss."

Aunt Rue smiled sadly. "Perhaps," she said, but her voice held no trace of hope. "Strange name for a tea that's supposed to bring on dreams, isn't it?"

Before Aunt Violet could reply, there was a loud knock on the door.

They both jumped at the sound.

"News," said Aunt Violet, her voice tremulous.

❖❖❖❖❖❖

Standing at the door—two children and a woman underneath a large black umbrella.

"Good evening. I'm Hester Bain, and this is my daughter Beatriz and my son Phinneas," said the woman.

"Sophie's and Wil's new friends," said Aunt Rue, as she welcomed them into the kitchen. "But to meet under such circumstances…"

"Hardly easy, I know," said Mrs. Bain, and she shook out her umbrella on the porch steps. "I hope you don't mind our dropping in like this." Her eyes fell on the dragonfly cake with the birthday candles on it. "Phinneas and Beatriz told me it's Sophie's and Wil's birthday today," she said.

"Yes," said Aunt Rue sadly, as she pulled up extra chairs to the table. "I'm Sophie's and Wil's Aunt Rue, and this is their Aunt Violet." She gestured to the table in the living room. "They haven't even seen their presents," she said, her voice breaking. "We just can't understand what's happened."

"Would you like a cup of tea, or a few biscuits?" asked Aunt Violet.

"Thank you, no," said Mrs. Bain firmly, before Phinneas and Beatriz could say anything. "It's quite late and the children will be going to bed soon."

At the look of disappointment on Aunt Violet's face—not to mention Phinneas's and Beatriz's faces—Mrs. Bain said hastily, "Well, I'm sure one biscuit would be lovely."

Aunt Violet offered Beatriz and Phinneas the platter of chocolate whiz biscuits. "I made them in case Sophie and Wil—" she said. She swallowed and sat back down at the table.

"The Firecatchers were thorough in their questioning," said Mrs. Bain. "And the children were understandably nervous—the Firecatchers are intimidating. Although it's late and the children are tired, we thought you would like to hear from the children themselves what happened. The authorities seem as puzzled as we are."

"The Firecatchers have assured us they're doing everything they can to sort out exactly what happened," said Aunt Rue.

"Unfortunately, it's not the first time something has happened to the children," said Aunt Violet. "The snakes of Narcisse…" Her voice trailed off.

"Yes, I know it must not be easy for you," said Mrs. Bain. "We read about the snakes of Narcisse and the Serpent's Chain in the paper."

"Beatriz and Phinneas, why don't you tell the Isidors—I mean, Aunt Rue and Aunt Violet—what happened," said Mrs. Bain.

"You've probably told everyone what you remember, children," Aunt Rue encouragingly, "but maybe there's something else we're missing."

"We…we were sitting in the greenhouse at Gruffud's eating our picnic," said Beatriz.

"The small greenhouse," added Phinneas.

"And we were playing a game," said Beatriz.

"What kind of game?" asked Aunt Violet.

"A word game," said Phinneas.

"Wil looked up some words in his notebook," said Beatriz.

"And Mage Radix said they were the names of New Zealand honey, really popular ones," said Phinneas.

"There were four names, one for each of us," said Beatriz.

"Which ones were they?" asked Aunt Rue.

"*Tawari, kamahi*—said Phinneas. He paused, trying to think.

"—*manuka, pohutukawa*," said Beatriz.

"Yes, all nice New Zealand honeys," said Aunt Violet. "We've tried every single one of them."

"And we pretended they were the words in a magic spell to tell the future," said Beatriz.

Aunt Violet looked extremely interested in this. "Saying the words would help you tell the future?" she asked.

"Not exactly," said Beatriz, biting her lip. "You had to say them at the same time as you bit into the honey sandwich."

"Bea and I said the words," said Phinneas, "and we had our eyes closed."

"You had to close your eyes?" asked Aunt Rue.

"Yes, or it wouldn't work properly," said Beatriz.

"Sophie and Wil closed their eyes too," said Phinneas, "and they were supposed to take a bite of the honey sandwich."

"So you didn't see what happened then, either of you?" asked Aunt Rue.

"We closed our eyes and said the words," said Beatriz.

"And when we opened them," said Phinneas, "they were… they were—"

"—gone," said Beatriz.

"Gone," repeated Aunt Rue, her voice flat.

"What kind of honey was it?" asked Aunt Violet sharply.

"I don't know. Just plain honey, I think," said Beatriz.

"We didn't get a chance to try it," said Phinneas.

"And the Firecatchers took the whole picnic basket," said Beatriz. "I guess they're checking everything in it."

"Where did you get the honey?" asked Aunt Rue. "Was it from Mage Radix?"

"Sophie and Wil brought it," said Phinneas. "It was in the picnic basket."

"It must have been the honey I pulled out of the cupboard," said Aunt Violet. "One of those jars we got at the Dragonfly Festival at Flavia Bottle's honey tent, remember Rue?"

"Yes, the day Lucretia Daggar was there," said Aunt Rue slowly, her eyes thoughtful. "Do you think the honeys on the counter could have gotten mixed up—maybe Sophie or Wil picked up the wrong jar?"

"What do you mean, Rue?" asked Aunt Violet.

"Why would it make a difference?" asked Mrs. Bain.

"I'm not sure," said Aunt Rue. "But those are four quite ordinary words, aren't they?"

"Is there anything else you can tell us children?" asked Mrs. Bain.

"I noticed—" Bea said, but she stopped.

"What did you notice, dear?" asked Mrs. Bain. "No matter how trifling the detail, it may be important. Try and remember."

"There were lots of rainbows," said Beatriz.

"What rainbows?" asked Phinneas.

"Didn't you see them, Phinn?" asked Beatriz. "Every time the dragonflies flashed by the window, there were dozens of rainbows in the greenhouse. It was so beautiful."

"Do the Firecatchers know about the dragonflies?" asked Aunt Rue. Mrs. Bain, Aunt Rue and Aunt Violet exchanged dark looks.

"Do you think Sophie and Wil will ever come back?" asked Phinneas.

"What if they never left?" said Aunt Rue slowly. "What if they were there with you all along?"

"What in snake's breath are you talking about, Rue?" asked Aunt Violet.

"That was probably no ordinary honey," said Aunt Rue. *"Apis mellifera—"* She stopped abruptly. "I'm sorry, I can't tell you."

"Why not?" asked Aunt Violet.

"The Secretariat…it's classified information," said Aunt Rue, her forehead wrinkling.

"Oh, drat the Secretariat," said Aunt Violet. "Rue, the children need our help."

"They're our friends," said Phinneas and Beatriz together.

"They told us that Lucretia Daggar—the woman we bought our house from—was involved somehow," said Beatriz.

"And she was friends with Rufus Crookshank when they were young," said Phinneas.

Aunt Rue seemed to be having an argument with herself, but at the mention of Lucretia Daggar's name, she finally spoke. "Lucretia Daggar and Rufus Crookshank?" she repeated.

Phinneas and Beatriz nodded their heads.

Aunt Rue's lips tightened. "This would answer a lot of questions," she said bleakly. She took a deep breath. "All right, here it is. *Apis mellifera magykalis.*"

"What does that mean?" asked Beatriz.

"It's the scientific name for a magical honeybee. Rare—so rare, in fact, it was once thought those bees had died out long ago. According to our archives, it's believed one of the first keepers may have been a member of the Serpent's Chain, although we don't know for sure. When members of the Serpent's Chain were persecuted and died, their knowledge died with them, along with the bees. But it seems *apis mellifera magykalis* survived—not as a domesticated bee, but in the wild. According to the records, they were extremely difficult to domesticate in the first place. They hated captivity."

"But what's so special about these bees?" asked Mrs. Bain.

"It's not the bees so much as the honey they produce. It appears to have magical qualities," said Aunt Rue. "When it's fresh, red streaks run through it, but after it has aged, those streaks disappear; the honey is practically indistinguishable from, say, ordinary clover honey. Its distribution is highly regulated; in fact, it's illegal to sell it on the open market, with the result, of course, that people are willing to pay hundreds of doublers for it on the black market.

"What happens if you eat the honey?" asked Phinneas.

"Magic isn't always predictable," said Aunt Rue, "despite our best efforts to turn it into a formulaic science. The *magykalis* honey is purported to give those who consume it powers of transformation and foreknowledge. But my understanding is that not just anyone can eat the honey. Some believe it is also a poisonous killing honey and say only those whom the bees trust may partake of it safely—others, they say, will come to a sorry end. And with that trust, the honey is reputed to give special knowledge about the future.

"This is dangerous honey. We don't even really know what quantity is safe to ingest—especially for children. It probably affects different people differently. I don't know what rainbows would have to do with it, but remember the Brimstone Snakes only acted as a portal to Narcisse when there was a rainbow in the sky. At any rate, it would take a powerful spell to transform—the honey alone probably wouldn't do it.

"We don't know if they ate some of the *magykalis* honey. If they did, then they may have been transformed. They may have been right there in the greenhouse with you, but you didn't see them. Where they are now is anyone's guess."

"But we've got to find them," said Phinneas.

"Were there any bees in the greenhouse when you had your picnic?" asked Aunt Rue, gazing intently at each of the children in turn.

'I can't remember," said Phinneas, shaking his head.

"I can't remember either," said Beatriz.

"After we said the words," said Phinneas, "it went all quiet in the greenhouse."

"There was a cricket chirping from somewhere and all those dragonflies were there," added Beatriz.

"But were there any bees?" persisted Aunt Rue.

"We don't know," the children answered, both of them on the verge of tears.

"It certainly is late, everyone," said Aunt Violet, her eyes watering. "Why don't you take these biscuits home with you, children? No sense in wasting them. And you've barely touched them with all this…all this…upsetness…"

"Don't worry," said Aunt Rue. "Sophie and Wil will come home soon. And then you can join us for their birthday celebration, all right?"

Beatriz and Phinneas both nodded, their faces tear-stained.

❖❖❖❖❖❖

Aunt Violet sighed and carefully wrapped up the *BUZzz* crystal ball in an old piece of flannel and placed the bundle underneath her bed. She eyed the small notebook and pen on her bedside table, as she poured tea into an old yellow teacup with a chipped handle.

"Dreamnought tea, we've got some work ahead of us tonight, you and I," she said.

Nimbus, cirrus, stratus, scud
Vanquish haze, mist, smog and mud
Mare's tail, mackerel sky
Lest hope fail, lest hope die.

The yellow teacup was not yet drained, when Aunt Violet yawned, blew out the lamp and closed her eyes; before you could have said *a stitch, a snitch, a switch, the ditch,* she was sound asleep and snoring fitfully.

XXİV Code Ƶ

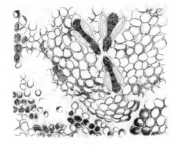

Hark! Clean, Lick and Comb Our Precious Shining Waxen Dome.

DOMUS DULCIS DOMUS
HOME SWEET HOME

In the fading light, high above the stone Entrance to the City of Wax, a Tablet inscribed with luminescent words…

ONE FOR ALL, AND ALL FOR ONE

Wil found the Sentiment strangely comforting.

His Fur bristled, however, at the sight of a dozen ferocious Bees all standing high on their back four Feet at the Entrance. They flicked their Antennae and clicked their Wings angrily at the Smell of Sophie and Wil.

Sentries, he thought, trembling at their huge, unblinking Eyes. Their Faces were as menacing as the one he had seen in the Crystal Ball.

Day's End, Long Live the Queen, Long Reign She O'er Us, buzzed the largest Sentry. She waited for a Reply.

When Wil and Sophie didn't answer quickly enough, the Sentries opened their Mouths as wide as they could gape and unfurled their long, rasping, hairy Tongues. Their shimmering Wings fanned out and filled the Cave Entrance; Wil reeled from the sudden alarming Smell of *Alert! Threat! Vagabonds, Intruders, Trespassers!* slashing through the Air.

Bowing low and tucking their Abdomens in, Wil and Sophie, neither of them yet fluent in Bee-Tongue, buzz-bumbled *Long Live the Queen*—only to the human ear, it would have sounded like *Bzzzz, Bzzzz, Bzz, Bzzzzzzz.*

Friends or Foes? demanded the Sentries, lowering their Wings a Notch. *Friends,* said Sophie. *We Bring Gifts of Sweet.*

The Sentries' Antennae whisked quickly over the Pollen Sac on Sophie's Hind Leg and frisked the Bee-Fur on Wil's Abdomen, still sprinkled with Dragonspot Lily Pollen. Satisfied, the Sentries waved Sophie and Wil on and turned back to the Entrance.

Sophie and Wil bowed low in Gratitude and cleaned their Antennae before proceeding into the Great Hall. The Smell of Mother-of-Us-All and the Smells of Thousands of her Offspring filled the Great Hall. The Smell was hard to describe, but it was a little like the Smell of a favourite, soft Blanket, comforting and reassuring. Every Corner of the Hive was alive with Hurry and Bustle—Brood-Keepers poking and prodding, feeding and cleaning their Cradlebrood, Wax-Makers building their Ladders and Gangways, *Sweet*-Masters fanning *Sweet* Chambers, Cleaners, Builders, Gatherers, Sculptors, Architects, Sentries, all buzzbusy with their appointed Tasks.

Yet amidst the Hurry and Bustle, Wil felt soothed by the Order and Rhythm of the Honeycomb—neat Chamber after Chamber, Row after Row, some capped, others open and brimming with Pollen Splashes of Yellow, Orange, Mauve, and Black. Smells filled his Antennae—the Scents of *Sweet*—so beguiling, it was easy to forget All Else. *Sweet* from Acres of Clover, Sniffs of Lavender, Roadside Wildflowers, Fields of Spring Dandelions, Sunflowers warmed in the Sun, Boughs heavy with Apple Blossoms…and Others he did not recognize immediately.

Chant after Chant pulsed through his Antennae and filled his Head—thousands of Bees were buzzsinging in Harmony together. Some of the Buzzes sounded like Orders…

Hark! Clean, Lick and Comb
Our Precious Shining Waxen Dome.

...and others sounded like Lungfelt Prayers of Thanks.

Thanks Be to the Mother-of-Us-All,
She-Who-Obeys-and-Is-Obeyed,
Queen of the Dark, Rejoice!
For Our Larders of Sweet Sweet Be Plenty,
Our Nurseries Brim with Shining Brood.
Through Months of Cold Moons Soon-to-Come
Yet Shall We Shall Live, Yet Shall We Live.
So Say We As One, So Say We As All.
Sweet, Sweet, Sweet.

One of the Sister Bees stopped and offered him regurgitated *Sweet* from her Bee-Gut and he slurped hungrily—for as a Drone, he was unable to feed himself—until he had had his Fill, while Sophie sipped happily from one of the *Sweet* Chambers with her long Tongue.

Just as the Sister Bee moved off to tend to another Task, a loud, raucous Transmission shouted over the Antennawire—

Emergency Alert. Code Z. STOP.
Impostors and Intruders.
Emergency Alert. Code Z. STOP.
Impostors and Intruders.
To the Cave Entrance
TOUT DE SUITE, TOUT DE SUITE.

Wil turned his Head and gazed across the Honeycomb towards the Entrance. A Rogue-Bee was sneaking into the Great Nest—a Rogue-Bee whose Head Fur was worn bare. Its jagged Wings juddered, *Buz-z-z-z-z-z-z-z.*

Wil's Antennae tingled and his Bee Gut tightened at the Sight of it. Its Presence was *Not Sweet*. In a wrenching Flash of Recognition, Wil realized the Rogue-Bee was Rufus Crookshank.

As if smelling Wil's Bee-Thoughts, Sophie buzzed quietly, *Crookshank.*

The Sentries must have also thought the Rogue-Bee's Presence was *Not Sweet,* for they surrounded him, waved their Antennae threateningly and demanded he give an Account of himself.

Rogue-Bee bowed low and held out his front Legs, which were covered in Bee Pollen. The Sentries buzzed among themselves...

Friend or Foe, Friend or Foe,
Sweet, Not Sweet
We Cannot Tell, We Do Not Know.

...until they were distracted by the arrival of another Bee, this one with Stripes of Black and pale White. Pale-Bee quickly shielded Rogue-Bee.

Daggar, Sophie buzzed, but her buzz sounded strangled.

Trouble, Wil buzzed back.

Pale-Bee was carrying a large Basket of Nectar and Pollen on her hind Leg. She circled around the Guards and buzzed loudly

Sweet, Sweet, Sweet.
Come One, Come All
to Sweet, Sweet, Sweet.

Her Dancing of beating Wings became more urgent; she spun around and sent out a high-pitched Buzz. Sister Bees stretched out their Antennae and touched her Abdomen. Pale-Bee whirled again in a small Circle for what seemed like a long Time (in human time, it would probably have been no more than a minute). The Sister Bees whirled after her in a Frenzy; Moments later they rushed out of the Great Nest to search for the newfound *Sweet*—for the Dance must have told them it was Nearby—leaving behind Rogue-Bee and Pale-Bee.

As their enormous unblinking Eyes fastened on Wil and Sophie, Wil's Antennae prickled and stood on End. He felt his Chest Fur thicken; it was glowing brightly.

XXV Freedom's Perfume

Fly! she buzzed.

FREMITE BELLUM, PROELIUM, VIRES.
DEFENDITE PUGNAM, PROPOSITUM, VITAM.
ROAR WAR, FIGHT AND MIGHT.
THE END, DEFEND, TO LIFE AND STRIFE.

Sophie looked at Wil, whose Bee-Fur was standing on End. He was at least twice his usual Drone Size; and there was a Patch of glowing Fur on his Chest.

Out! she buzzed.

Trapped, he answered in a low, growling Buzz.

Rogue-Bee and Pale-Bee began to creep around to the Side of the Hive where Sophie and Wil were crouching.

Sophie's Bee-Guts clenched. *Fly!* she buzzed.

But a loud, raucous, euphoric Party of Sister Bees zoomed back into the Great Nest. They were laden with fresh *Sweet*, their Fur brushed with Rain Drizzle. Wild with the wealth of *Sweet* they had uncovered, they tumbled and bumbled over each other, buzzing noisily, *Never-Shall-We-Want-For-Golden-Blessings-Come-To-Be.*

So noisy and disorderly were they that they spilled over Rogue-Bee and Pale-Bee.

Bee-Breath! buzzed Wil loudly to Sophie. ("Quick!" in human-tongue.) *Make Tracks!*

But the disorderly Party of Sister Bees had quite blocked the Entrance to the Great Nest.

Like some maddened Bull intent on escaping its Pen, Wil zoomed full Tilt at the Sister Bees, pushing Several of them aside.

Sophie! he buzzed.

But the small Opening he managed to dash through closed in after him at once.

❖❖❖❖❖❖

Sophie, alas, was left behind. Now she knew what Wil must have felt like when she had headed out from the Snake Dens at Narcisse, leaving him alone to face Rufus Crookshank.

Not waiting to see if Rogue-Bee and Pale-Bee had crawled out yet from under the Bee Party, she scuttled behind a Cluster of Sister Bees cleaning *Sweet* Chambers. She ducked through a Hole into another Sector near the Nursery. Creeping over the backs of Sister Bees and without looking behind her once, she crawled as quickly as she could far away from the Entrance. Her Lungs heaving, she soon found herself in an unfamiliar Part of the Hive—where the all-consuming Smell of Mother-of-Us-All soothed and smoothed her hackled Fur.

Twelve Sister Bees—the Retinue of Honour—were fussing over a Bee much larger than any Others. Her long, swollen, gleaming Abdomen glistened in the Half-Light, Half-Dark of the Great Nest.

Sophie felt Great Peace. She bowed low, her Antennae grazing the Honeycomb.

The memories of Pale-Bee and Rogue-Bee faded. They no longer mattered. There was much more important Business to take care of. Sophie inched her way into the Circle and began cleaning the hind Feet of Mother-of-Us-All, while Sister Bees caressed the Wings of Mother-of-Us-All and waved their Antennae over her as she slowly lowered her Body into one of the Cells…and deposited a single, radiant, glowing Egg.

How many Bee-Minutes or Bee-Hours passed, Sophie did not know, did not care, so diligently did she execute her Duties…until an unfamiliar Smell filled her Tongue. Mother-of-Us-All's Bee-Fur suddenly felt spiky and scratchy.

A new Message began—softly and steadily, at first…then louder and louder, until it ended in a Banshee Bee-Scream that shook Sophie's Bee-Soul.

No Life Without Strife
No Rights Without Fights
No Flight, We Fight
Or the Bloom is Doomed
By Sun and Moon
Freedom's Perfume
War, Hear Us Roar
Defend to the End
Lunes, Oppugne, the Dance of the Runes
Mother-of-Us-All, Hear Our Call.

Sophie's Bee-Blood stirred at the Shriek of the Message (*Hear-and-Obey* in Bee-Tongue).

The words repeated and tumbled in on top of each other. *Roar War, Fight and Might, One for All and All for One, End, Defend, to Life and Strife.*

XXVI SHELTER in the STORM

"I think it's trying to tell us something, whoever it is," said Portius.

CERTO HOMO ES. QUID SPERABAS?
TE HABERE ALAS AETERNAS?
OF COURSE, YOU'RE HUMAN. WHAT DID YOU EXPECT?
THAT YOU WOULD HAVE WINGS FOREVER?

In his Haste to escape, Wil ploughed directly into the Hindquarters of one of the Sentries at the Cave Entrance.

Watch where you're going, growl-buzzed the Sentry. She clearly had no Inkling about the Disaster brewing within. *What are you doing?* she asked, adding in a perfunctory Way, *Hail Mother-of-Us-All.*

Wil buzzed—or perhaps hiccupped would be a better word, for Bees do hiccup sometimes, especially when they are nervous—*Hail Mother-of-Us-All,* he replied. Then he blurted out, *"Share-Scare!"* ("Help!" in human-tongue.)

The Sentry's Antennae waved in the air and crossed over each other, as if she were confused. Wil panicked and before the Sentry could question him further, he shot out of the Cave and bolted into the Night (*Sun-Under* in Bee-Tongue).

The Bee-Purple Sky shuddered, and the dark Night Clouds split open and turned themselves inside out. Great Belches of Raindrizzle soaked Wil's Bee-Fur and he cringed as Thunder rattled the Clouds. He could barely fly, let alone see where he was going, in the sopping Wet. He saw a faint Glow of Light below him and swerved towards it. With Relief, he realized he had unwittingly flown straight to the main Entrance of Big CombStone. He alighted on a Stone hidden underneath a Vine and pondered how to get in. Drops of Water slid down the Stone and soaked his Feet. He shivered.

The Door was firmly shut and there did not appear to be any Holes or Cracks. Lightning flashed so close his Bee-Fur tingled. He darted to the Door Handle and cowered underneath it, his five Eyes blind with Fright. Trying to calm himself, he took a deep Bee-Breath and cleaned his Antennae. When his Vision cleared, he saw a perfect Bee-Door right beside him, of such a Size that he could easily crawl through. (It was, of course, the keyhole.)

He quickly winged from the Bee-Door over to Portia and Portius. *Help*, he buzzed loudly. *Help!*

Portia and Portius appeared to be sound asleep, however. Not even one of their Snake Braids stirred.

He landed on Portia's nose and buzzed as loudly as he could.

Portia stirred but did not wake up.

Desperate, Wil flew over to Portius and buzzed from one Snake Braid to another in quick Succession.

❖❖❖❖❖❖

Portius opened one sleepy eye. "Hmmm...a bee," he said.

"What did you say?" murmured Portia without opening her eyes.

"It's a bee," said Portius, yawning.

"To be or not to be, that is the question," mumbled Portia. She yawned. "Why are you waking me up to talk about this?"

"Would you open your eyes, my dear Portia," said Portius. "Not that *be*. A *bee*...the one that's flying right past your nose at this very moment."

"Oh, a bee," said Portia carelessly. "Probably just seeking shelter in the storm." She opened one eye and yawned again. "Such a storm."

"Forget the storm," said Portius testily. "It's not acting like a regular bee."

Portia, suddenly alert, eyed the bee that was now circling around and around Portius's head. "What, or more to the point, *who* do you think it is?" she asked sharply. "Remember that Preying Mantis some fifty years ago?"

"Hmmm," said Portius, squinting cross-eyed up at the bee. "Remember like it was yesterday. Glowing green on the stone floor, its jaws chattering at us. Turned out to be a lost wizard who had been missing for a year, as I recall."

"Yes, that's the one. He'd completely forgotten how to transmutate back," said Portia. "Got stuck."

"Very sad," said Portius. "Didn't they take him to the MiddleGate Sanatorium? Quite some time to bring him back, as I recall. But he was never right in the head again. Humans have to be careful how long they stay in that transmutation state, or the temporary becomes permanent."

"But what about this little beastie?" said Portia. "It does seem desperate, doesn't it? Do you think we know it?"

"I think it's trying to tell us something, whoever it is," said Portius.

A jolt of lightning lit the foyer up as though it were broad daylight. The unearthly light danced on the stained glass window above Portia's and Portius's heads; a prism jewel at window's centre twinkled and a rainbow flashed right onto the centre of Portius's forehead. The small bee was wrapped in a rainbow cloak for one brief moment.

✦✦✦✦✦✦

Wil felt his Bee-Fur melt away from him. His five Eyes became two and his Antennae disappeared. Six legs became two, his wings dissolved and he tumbled to the floor, his awkward, heavy limbs flailing.

"S-s-snake's b-b-blood!" he exclaimed. His tongue felt thick and leathery. "H-h-human again."

"Wil Wychwood, welcome. Of course you're human," said Portius wryly. "What did you expect? That you would have wings forever?"

"How kind of you to drop in, Mr. Wychwood," said Portia graciously and with no hint of surprise in her voice.

"T-t-t-trouble," Wil stammered. "They're going to d-d-destroy the bees."

Portia and Portius closed their eyes and intoned together:

Honey wonder, honey plunder
Never fear for they will blunder
Hum bees roar bees
Stone split thunder sunder
Stone split thunder sunder.

Then Portia and Portius shuddered, as if realizing the all-too-dreadful meaning of their stony words.

But before Wil could ask any questions, he felt his arms and legs tingling. Bee-Fur, scratchy and warm, covered his Chest. He fell to his Knees and his two Legs multiplied by three. He seemed to shrink as the Hall grew larger and larger. His Antennae re-appeared and he could hear a Message, faint though it was—a Message that chilled his Bee-Blood. *Roar War, Fight and Might, One for All and All for One, End, Defend, to Life and Strife.*

He saw Portia's and Portius's Mouths moving—only now he thought of their Mouths as two deep, dark Holes. Deep Growls—Sounds he did not understand—roared out of the Holes.

Terrified, he fled through the Bee-Door back out into the cold, wet Darkness, not knowing where he was going or what he was doing. The Thunder was so loud, Wil thought surely the Sky was clearing its Throat and its rumbling Abdomen was about to eat him up. His Antennae curled up in Fright. Another bolt of Lightning pierced the Sky and the *End-Defend* Message finished abruptly. Wil plummeted to the Ground, senseless, his Bee-Fur so drenched he could easily have been mistaken for a Clot of Mud.

XXVII Aunt Violet's Dream

The pen was leaking ink, as if it too were crying.

QUAM DAEMONES DUBITATIONIS
NOS SOLLICITANT MEDIA IN NOCTE.
HOW THE DEMONS OF DOUBT
PLAGUE US IN THE NIGHT.

Flashes of lightning lit the wall of Aunt Violet's bedroom and deep thunder rattled the window panes. Aunt Violet was having a restless sleep—at least, whatever sleep she could steal with so many trips to the bathroom. It was still the stormy middle of the night when she awoke yet again, this time from a dream. Shivering and yawning, she lit her lamp and fumbled for the notebook and pen on her bedside table.

"Where are you when I need you, you wretched pen?" she muttered. "You were right here. You don't think my dreams are important enough to write down, do you? I have half a mind to throw you out when I do find you. I shan't give you the pleasure of knowing what my dream was anyway.

"That stupid tea. I must have put too much mugwort in it; maybe I was only supposed to put in half the amount, or maybe I added two parts instead of one part." She held her head in her hands. Still grumbling to herself, she managed to find her pen, which had fallen to the floor.

She squinted ruefully at the pen. "Don't try that again, or I really will throw you out." She opened the notebook and began to write, speaking under her breath as the pen scratched across the paper and blotted letters here and there.

I was running out in the garden in my dressing gown. My hair wasn't purple any more. It was bright yellow.

"What a funny idea! Sophie and Wil might have to call me Aunt Lemon instead." She eyed a large ink splotch between the words bright and yellow. "Aunt Lemon doesn't have quite the ring to it that Aunt Violet does." She shook the pen and exclaimed, "You wretched pen, if you don't start behaving…" She left the threat unspoken this time, but as if the pen had now decided to behave, the ink began to flow smoothly.

Cyril's gargoyle was trying to tell me something and its mouth was opening and closing, as if it were talking. But no words were coming out. I tried to speak but no words came out of my mouth either.

When I touched the gargoyle, it screamed—but it screamed without making a sound (I knew it was screaming though). And its tail, instead of being in a spiral, had come all unwound.

Then I dreamt I was a little girl again. I ran so quickly that my feet left the ground and I was flying through the air. I was flying higher and higher and higher, almost as high as the sun.

A black cloud covered the sun and I fell down into a hole in the ground.

"Well, a flying dream is a good dream, isn't it? But what does it mean? I'm too addled to know."

She sniffed and hunted about for a handkerchief, to no avail. Trying to stem the dam of tears, she pulled up her flannel sheet and dabbed at her eyes, failing to notice the pen was leaking ink, as if it too were crying.

"Here you have a crystal ball, which you hardly know how to use. The tea leaves are a waste of time and your dreams are no help at all in finding Sophie and Wil. You ridiculous old woman, go back to sleep."

XXVIII The Chandelier Plan

The storm was loud enough to wake up the entire world.

UNUM CONSILIUM NULLO CONSILIO PRAESTAT;
AT QUOD SI CONSILIUM MALUM SIT?
IT'S BETTER TO HAVE A PLAN THAN NO PLAN AT ALL;
BUT WHAT IF THE PLAN TURNS OUT TO BE A BAD PLAN?

❝Pssst. Bea, are you awake?" whispered Phinneas.

"Hmmm," answered Beatriz, pulling her covers up over her head.

Phinneas yanked the covers back. "Bea, wake up."

Beatriz sat bolt upright, blinking sleepily. "What's the matter?" She squinted at her brother, who was standing fully dressed beside her bed. He was wild-eyed and his hair was so rumpled he must have just tumbled out of bed.

Are you sleepwalking?" she asked.

"No. I'm awake," he whispered, "and I've got an idea."

"What are you talking about?" said Beatriz, feeling irked, for she had just been in the middle of a nice dream about bicycling across a bridge to an ice cream store. "What time is it?" she asked. "It's still dark outside."

"It's four o'clock," said Phinneas in a matter-of-fact way, as though he were in the habit of waking up at that hour. "Ssshhh, or you'll wake Mum up—although I suppose we don't have to worry. The storm's loud enough to wake up the entire world. Look, I have an idea."

"Idea?" asked Beatriz, trying to sound interested when all she really wanted to do was sink back under her warm covers.

"Yeah. How we're going to save Wil and Sophie. I've got to show you something."

At the mention of Sophie and Wil, Beatriz hopped out of bed without another word of protest and followed Phinneas. They tiptoed down the hallway.

"Where are we going?" she asked.

"Downstairs."

A great clap of thunder set Beatriz's heart racing. "I hope your idea doesn't involve going outside," she said.

Phinneas didn't answer. Instead, he crept into the dining room and pointed at the ceiling.

"What's so important about the ceiling?" asked Beatriz impatiently.

"Not the ceiling," said Phinneas, speaking slowly as if she were completely dense. "The chandelier."

"Okay, it's a chandelier," said Beatriz, "but you didn't have to wake me up to show it to me. I've seen it already."

"All right," said Phinneas, sounding hard done by. "If you don't want to help—"

"Of course, I want to help," snapped Beatriz. "It's partly our fault. We said those words."

"Aunt Rue said the words probably had nothing to do with it," said Phinneas. "But the rainbows are probably an important part of the spell. And we were there all together. So we're part of it. Besides, they're our friends."

"And we have no idea where they are," said Beatriz.

"I think they did turn into bees," said Phinneas.

"But we don't know for sure," said Beatriz. "Remember Aunt Rue said the honey probably couldn't actually transform people by itself, and she should know because she works at the Secretariat."

"Well, I think they *did* turn into bees," repeated Phinneas. "We just didn't look around us carefully enough. We have to go Gruffud's and—"

"—stand there in the dark waiting for them to fly by? Is that your idea? Because if it is, count me out," said Beatriz.

"Oh, come on, Bea. It's more complicated than that. We're going to take some of the crystals from the chandelier with us."

"Now what are you talking about?" asked Beatriz. Of all the snake-legged schemes Phinneas had ever come up with, this was undoubtedly the worst.

"They'll make rainbows, of course," said Phinneas. "Without rainbows, Wil and Sophie probably won't be able to change back into human form."

"Rainbows?" asked Beatriz. "In the dark?"

"No, of course not," said Phinneas. "But we'll get there just as the sun is coming up, and the light will flash through the prisms."

"And magically, somehow, Wil and Sophie will just fly by, while we're standing there holding up these dangly crystals?" said Beatriz sarcastically. "Is that what you think? We might as well take that dead dragonfly I have in the jar with us while we're at it."

"Good idea, Bea. Maybe it will bring us good luck," said Phinneas. "I should have thought of it."

"I wasn't serious," said Beatriz.

"Which ones shall we take?" asked Phinneas, looking up at the chandelier speculatively, like a magpie inspecting a prized collection of stolen blue beads. He seemed completely oblivious to Beatriz's grumpiness.

"The big ones ought to make the best rainbows," he said enthusiastically. "I'll pass them down to you. We have to be careful they don't drop, or Mum will have a snake."

"I don't think this is a good idea," Beatriz said. "What if we lose one? Or it breaks?"

Phinneas didn't answer. He was too busy trying to pick up one of the chairs. It was much too heavy for one person to move.

"All right," said Beatriz with a sigh, and together, they managed to drag the chair over without scraping the floor.

Phinneas clambered up and reached for one of the prisms.

"Not the largest one, Phinn," whispered Beatriz. "That one's right in the middle. Mum will notice it's missing. Take one from each side, so it looks symmetrical. Take four. There were four words and four of us."

"You're right," said Phinneas. He reached for one of the smaller prisms. "It's just attached with a bit of wire."

"Careful. You're leaning to one side. Don't pull on it, or the whole thing will come down!" said Beatriz, trying hard to whisper.

"Got it," said Phinneas triumphantly. He slid the crystal into Beatriz's hand. It was cold and smooth. She held it up. A flash of lightning caught its facets, and it seemed to light up from within.

"This ought to work really well," she said. "But I still don't see how our standing out in a field somewhere at Gruffud's and holding up these crystals in the air is going to do anything."

Phinneas slid another crystal into her hand.

"We'll figure something out when we get there," he said. "If you plan everything beforehand, then..."

"Then what?" said Beatriz. "It's better to have a plan than no plan at all."

"Well, you might...you might miss an opportunity," said Phinneas, "if you're too busy following your plan. And what if the plan is a bad plan?"

"Well, I'm not going out in any storm," said Beatriz.

XXIX THE GREAT CIRCLE

Hold Belly-Close Yonder Blue Sky.

PUGNA PUGNATA EST PRIUSQUAM COEPERIT.
THE BATTLE WAS OVER BEFORE IT BEGAN.

The rosy fingers of dawn were just beginning to curl over the horizon. The thunderstorm seemed to have grudgingly given way to a dark grey drizzle of rain, as if refusing to relinquish its hold on MiddleGate entirely. Thunder rumbled in the distance and there were puddles everywhere. The bees were just beginning to stir inside the belly of the stone gargoyle atop Gruffud's.

The new Shift of Sentries shivered by the Entrance to the City of Wax, conferring with those just coming off the Night Shift.

"Hail. Night's End, Long Live the Queen, Long Reign She O'er Us, buzzed one of the Sentries from the new Shift. All the Sentries buzzed in Chorus. *"One-for-All-and-All-for-One."*

One of the Night Shift Sentries ran down the Checklist quickly, as if impatient to leave and get some Wing-Rest. *Not Sweet Rain all Night. Nest Safe. Queen Safe. Sweet Safe. Nothing New to report other than four Visitors. They brought Gifts of Sweet. Permitted Entry. One Visitor (Crazy Bee) left. Three remained.*

✦✦✦✦✦✦

Sophie stirred from behind the Wall of newly-laid Wax Honeycomb. She stretched her front Legs and yawned, forgetting where she was until she felt the Sun-Up Hum, as several thousand Bees around her slowly stretched their Wings and began to groom themselves for the Morning Sun Salutation. The Great Nest felt cool and damp. It must have rained during the Night.

Sophie cleaned her Antennae and tried to think clearly. Wil must have escaped and gone to get Help. He would be back soon…she hoped.

But what about those other two bees, Rogue-Bee and Pale-Bee? Were they still in the Great Nest? Sophie cleaned her Antennae again and began to comb the Fur on her back Legs. *If they were still in here, the Great Nest could be in danger.*

And if she tried to escape, what would happen to the Great Nest? What would happen to Mother-of-Us-All? The thought of something happening to Mother-of-Us-All was inconceivable. Without Mother-of-Us-All, the reason for…

Sophie did not have a chance to complete her Thought, for a powerful Smell touched her Antennae. *Something-Dangerous-This-Way-Comes. Something-Dangerous-This-Way-Comes,* repeated the message.

Sophie felt the Sister Bees around her tense. She heard several of them buzz *Frass* (which in human-tongue means insect excrement)— as close to Swearing as she ever heard while she lived among the Bees.

The Buzzing in the Great Nest increased suddenly and Wings began to flex. A new Message *(Hear-and Obey)* came as the Fur on Thousands of Bees bristled.

For Mother-of-Us-All, Sisters, Amass
Materfamilias, Bataillon En Masse
Shun, Outrun, Stun, We're Done
Foregone, We Die
Sine Qua Non

Like the Myrmidon
Die We as One

The Sisters turned to face *Something-Dangerous-This-Way-Comes.*

Sophie peered around from behind the Wall of new Wax. It was Rogue-Bee and Pale-Bee. *They're looking for Wil and me,* she thought. *We've put the Great Nest in Danger.*

She slowly crawled forwards to the front of the Bee-Line, buzz-murmuring, *One-for-All-and-All-for-One,* but Rogue-Bee and Pale-Bee seemed to shrink at the Sight of the Sisters rallied in Battle Formation.

They turned quickly and were gone in a Bee-Moment. The Battle was over before it began.

The Sisters sang a jubilant Buzz-Song as they danced in a Great Circle.

Mother-of-Us-All, Be Safe
Onward Sisters, Courage and Patience
Fly We Proud and Free.
Hold Belly-Close Yonder Blue Sky
Bribery, Roguery, Witchery Defy
Treachery, Trumpery, Sorcery, Usury
Jiggery-pokery, nolite-nos-tangere.

Sophie hastened to join in the Circle.

⬥⬥⬥⬥⬥⬥

"That was Rue Isidor's niece in there, I'm sure of it," said Lucretia Daggar. She stepped back from the edge of Gruffud's roof. "But I didn't see the drone Wil Wychwood anywhere. He may have have escaped," said Lucretia Daggar.

"We need that black medallion," said Rufus Crookshank.

"I know," said Lucretia Daggar. "But we have to be careful. We can't let anything happen to that Isidor girl. The Secretariat would launch a full investigation—especially as her aunt works there. There would be far too many questions. We can't take the chance. Without the status my position at the Secretariat confers, we would not as easily be able to advance the cause of the Serpent's Chain…and, my dear Rufus, your hard-won freedom would be in jeopardy."

Rufus Crookshank was silent. Then, his voice harsh, he said, "Forget the Secretariat. With control of the *magykalis* honey and the medallion, they will not be able to touch us. The Serpent's Chain numbers are few, but we will grow with the black medallion."

"Do it then," said Lucretia Daggar.

Rufus Crookshank pulled out the star-shaped vial.

Lucretia Daggar nodded.

He pulled out the stopper and tipped the vial over the stone gargoyle. A dark cloud spilled out and swirled into the mouth of the gargoyle.

The humming of the bees lulled.

Silence.

"Long Live the Serpent's Chain, sweet Lucy," said Rufus Crookshank.

"Long Live the Serpent's Chain, dear Rufus," said Lucretia Daggar.

And together they whispered, *"Voco vinco volo."*

XXX Esme

He landed near a Patch of Queen Anne's Lace.

UMQUAM CREVISTI VESTIGIA
LATENTIA SAEPE PATENTIA?
HAVE YOU EVER NOTICED CLUES
ARE OFTEN HIDDEN IN PLAIN SIGHT?

The storm clouds had begun their retreat. Large drops of water fell from leaves into puddles below. The skies began to turn the rosy pink of dawn's coming, like the rose petals strewn before a bride's procession.

Wil dragged himself painfully out of the Mud. Although it was still dark, he was able to see. The sound of chirping Monsters urged him to find a Hidey-Hole.

He crawled into the Shadow of a large Stone and tried to remember what had happened the Night before. Slowly, Memory returned to him. Portia and Portius. He had assumed human Form for a Bee-Moment, long enough to tell them the Bees were in Danger.

And Portia and Portius had told him Something—Something important—but what?

And Sophie, where was Sophie? Wil stroked his right Antenna, which was bent, and tried to remember. He heard the faintest Transmission repeating over and over in his Head...*Die We As One, Die We As One.*

Sophie was...she was still in the Great Nest. And the Great Nest was in Danger. He had to help.

⬥⬥⬥⬥⬥⬥

Aunt Violet padded into the kitchen in her dressing gown, her eyes bleary and puffy. A single candle cast a small but warm glow over the table. Aunt Rue was sitting there, sipping a cup of tea.

"That wretched tea did not work, Rue. I've been up and down all night," said Aunt Violet. "There must have been too much mugwort in it. And with the storm, how could anyone get a decent night's sleep anyway?"

"You look like you've had quite a night. I couldn't sleep either," said Aunt Rue. "I won't offer you any more tea, as I'm sure you've had quite enough of it," she added wryly.

"No word about the children?" asked Aunt Violet.

"None."

"You don't suppose they were out in the storm, do you?"

Aunt Rue did not answer.

"Well, I did have one dream," said Aunt Violet.

Aunt Rue looked up hopefully at Aunt Violet.

"And I tried to write it down...but I can't read a word of it this morning. It's gibberish—something about bees and flying. And the pen leaked all over the notebook. So I can't read a thing. The worst night I've had in years."

"I'm sorry," said Aunt Rue. "And unfortunately, Lucretia Daggar wants me to come to the office right away. There's some kind of emergency. Another one. I can't think what she wants. Doesn't that woman ever stop working?"

"Surely she must know the children are missing, Rue," said Aunt Violet. "How could she possibly expect you to go into work?"

"I don't know, but it must be something important," said Aunt Rue. "I'll try and be back as quickly as I can."

With Aunt Rue gone, Aunt Violet stared at the plate of buttered toast sitting on the table. Half-heartedly, she took a piece and spread wild blueberry jam on it. She took one bite; it tasted like cardboard.

Absent-mindedly, she shooed a bee away from the candle. "Scat, get away from there. Be careful, or you'll land in the wax or worse, singe your wings." She took a clean glass from the cupboard and trapped the bee against the window and covered the glass with one of her lacy handkerchiefs. Opening the window, she threw the bee outside.

"There you go, back where you belong, little bee," she said.

She sighed and sat back down at the table, staring out the dark window. The dawn sky glowed orange as fire.

❖❖❖❖❖❖

Wil found himself spinning through the Air. He landed near a Patch of Queen Anne's Lace. Aunt Violet had just quite unceremoniously pitched him out through the Clear.

Now what? he thought, as he circled around the Gargoyle (*Stone-Tail* in Bee-Tongue). It eyed him as suspiciously as it had when he was in human Form. Ignoring the Gargoyle's Scowl, he landed on top if its Head for a Bee-Moment. Looking down he saw one of the Quail Eggs nestled inside the Gargoyle's coiled Tail. He sighed a small Bee-Sigh and thought once again about Esme. He'd never see her again.

But at that moment, he caught a Movement from the Corner of his prismed Eye. What had just darted out from underneath the Stone Gargoyle?

Wil swooped down and perched near the Egg.

Something was there. He knew it. There was a familiar Smell. He cleaned his Antennae and waited.

He saw it cautiously peeping out from the dim Shadows underneath the Gargoyle.

There it was again.

Esme.

Wil could not believe his five Eyes.

Esme was hiding underneath the Gargoyle. She must have been hiding there all Summer.

He was so excited he flew around the Gargoyle in seven Circles before landing on top of the Gargoyle's Head again.

Esme, I can't touch you, but I'm here. It's me...Wil. It's me!

Esme glided out from the Shadows. If Wil wasn't mistaken, she looked right straight up at him. Then she did the Extraordinary.

She stretched out full-length, absolutely ramrod straight like one of the Snowsnakes at Winterlude Carnival. She was an Arrow, her Head pointing to the Great Nest.

Wil understood immediately. With one last grateful Circle around the Gargoyle, he sped back to the Great Nest as fast as he could fly.

XXXİ Stupour

The raccoon padded happily across the roof of the school.

NUMQUAM CONCEDITE!
NEVER SURRENDER!

Wil searched desperately inside the Great Nest for Sophie. He finally found her deep inside, huddled in a large, frozen Circle of Bees. She was staring catatonically, as were the Others, all of them seemingly unable to lift even one Antenna, one Leg.

All around them was sheer Devastation. Bees convulsed, their Legs twitching. Miraculously they were all Alive, but barely. A deep Cold filled his Abdomen, and if Bees had had Tears, Wil would have been weeping. The only Message going through his Head was bleak…

Never Surrender
Defend Our Splendour
Attack the Offender
Never Surrender…

The Message looped endlessly round and round until Wil thought he would surely go mad.

This wasn't Chalkbrood. This wasn't Fungus. It wasn't Phantom Mites. It wasn't even Moths. Wil knew there was a Cure for all those Things. This was far worse. If Wil could have put into human words what he understood...

A Cold Shadow comes over us.
It steals our Joy in Sweet.
We cannot move, such is our Lassitude.
We forget to take Care of our Young.
Our reason for Bee-ing leaves us.
The Cold Shadow robs us of our warm Darkness.
We are cold.
We lose all Hope and thus, dwindle into Nothingness.
The Cold Shadow swallows our Song.

❖❖❖❖❖❖

"Who's there?" asked Mage Radix. He held up a glowworm lantern and peered through the dim light at two figures lurking near the greenhouse. "Identify yourselves immediately, or I'll summon the Firecatchers."

"No need to summon anyone, Mage Radix," said a woman's voice from the shadows. "Lucretia Daggar from the Secretariat. Our apologies for disturbing you. I know it's an ungodly hour, but I'm here with Mr. Frank, my assistant."

"Oh," said Mage Radix, as he peered into the shadows. "Madame Daggar, I had no idea. We've had some suspicious goings-on the last while. There was a man said he was an Inspector with the Secretariat, but it turned out the Secretariat had no record of him. I told him to leave the property the last time I saw him. And I've been keeping an eye on the hives, just to make sure everything is all right. Don't want anything to go missing," he said pointedly.

"Perfectly understandable, Mage Radix," replied Lucretia Daggar, as she moved into the light of the glowworm lantern. "Thank you for your vigilance. I myself received a fresh report last night—nothing I'm able to share unfortunately—but I thought I'd better come and check things myself. You can only ask underlings—I mean, others—to do so much, you know."

"Yes, of course," said Mage Radix, and he bowed. "If you don't need my presence, I'll go and get some more shut-eye."

"I think we've mostly done what we came to do," said Lucretia Daggar, "right, Mr. Frank?"

Mr. Frank nodded without saying a word.

"Good," said Mage Radix with a curious glance at Mr. Frank. "It's been quite a responsibility, Madame Daggar," he added, "if you know what I mean."

"The Secretariat certainly appreciates your diligence, Mage Radix," said Lucretia Daggar. "As I'm sure you understand, we rely upon people such as yourself to ensure that...um...valuable resources are safe and do not fall into the wrong hands."

Mage Radix seemed pleased at these words. "I'll bid you good night—although I guess it will be morning soon enough!" He turned and trudged back to his quarters in the greenhouse, singing slightly off-key.

Au clair de la lune, mon ami Pierrot
Prête-moi ta plume, pour écrire un mot.
Ma chandelle est morte, je n'ai plus de feu.
Ouvre-moi ta porte, pour l'amour de Dieu.

He glanced up at the gargoyle on roof of the school, silhouetted against the pink sky; but it was still too dark for him to see the raccoon making its last foray of the night.

Nor, at such a distance, could he see two bees fly into the mouth of the gargoyle. And if he had looked behind him, he might have wondered how Madame Daggar and Mr. Frank had disappeared so quickly into the darkness.

❖❖❖❖❖❖

The raccoon padded happily across the roof of the school. It had been a good night. His belly was full. Soon it would be time to sleep, but the smell of something sweet had assailed his nostrils. It bore investigation.

The raccoon peered underneath the stone creature. A hole. Yes. That was it. The something sweet, something irresistible was inside. He was sure of it.

The raccoon had smelled honey before, but Mage Radix had made sure the repel charm around the hives was so strong that the raccoon had long ago given up even thinking about thinking about plundering the hives for their sweetness and chewy grubs.

But tonight was different. This was going to be easy. Who cared if he got stung a few times? The reward was too great.

His paw ever so delicately felt the lip of the gargoyle's mouth, the hole, then plunged inside. He pulled his paw out. It was coated with lovely, sticky sweetness.

Why were no stinging creatures defending it?

Not one to question so large a gift, the raccoon deftly inserted his paw again and pulled out a great gob of honeycomb. He discarded the few bees clinging to the honeycomb, having no interest in tangling with them, and munched to his heart's content on the honeycomb. Then, sated, he sauntered off towards his lair in the tower, just as the sun began to peep over the horizon.

❖❖❖❖❖❖

Wil stared in Horror at the great Paw that swiped at the Honeycomb and carried it away together with Sister Bees dangling from it.

ClawTooth, he thought (raccoon in human-tongue). The Great Nest will be destroyed. The Bees appeared to have lost all Strength to attack the Marauder.

Wil struggled to remember Something—that Something of Importance Portia and Portius had said. But what was it? He could hardly think with *Never Surrender, Defend Our Splendour, Attack the Offender, Never Surrender…* coursing endlessly through his Head.

What had the Bees told him? *The Shadow Swallows our Song.* That was it. The Great Nest was completely silent. No *Buzz.*

Now he remembered what Portia and Portius had said—

Hum Bees roar Bees
Stone split Thunder sunder

Wil began to hum a low, soft Buzz. *Loud,* he told himself. *Loud, so all the Bees will hear.* He took a deep Breath and with his every striped, lickety Ounce of Strength, he buzzed. His low Drone Buzz echoed in the Great Nest.

A Brother Drone beside him stirred from his stupour and started to hum.

A Sister Bee roused herself and buzzed, and the next and the next…until Hundreds, no Thousands of Bees were buzzing.

The Great Nest was filled again with deep, rumbling, Fur-shaking Sound—a sound that shook the belly of the gargoyle.

Beneath the Bee-Hum though, the Scent of another Message came unbidden. It was not a Message from the Mother-of-Us-All, She-Who-Obeys-and-Is-Obeyed. Wil was sure of that.

He tried to ignore the Scent, but it grew more insistent until a Smell exploded in his Bee-Veins.

To Those Who Doubt, to Those Who Sneered
The Serpent's Chain Has Disappeared
Hear and Fear, O Mighty Seer
For It Has Been Ordained
Unleashed on These Poor Innocents-s-s
The Serpent's Chain's Good Influence
Sincere, Corrupt and Utterly Profane
Await the Inexorable, the Right to Claim
The Return to Power, Hark the Hour
From Realms-s-s Unearthly, Realms-s-s of Myth
Follow the Path to the Z-Z-Zenith
In Cracks-s-s and Shadows-s-s They Have Survived
Hear, Then Fear, O Mighty Seer
For They Still Strive Link by Link
And Soon Will Thrive, Despite What Thou Think'st.

Even with the joyous Buzzhum of the Bees restored, Wil's Bee-Heart faltered at the chill Warning. Shaking his Bee-Body to rid himself of the poisonous Message, he turned to join the Circle of Bees beside Sophie. She buzzed a quick Note of Greeting and resumed her Buzzhumming along with the Others.

They did not notice a small Crack had suddenly appeared inside the Great Nest. Nor, with the now deafening Buzzroar did they yet sense two Bees advancing upon them, until Wil's Bee-Fur bristled. He looked down at his Chest. It was glowing brightly. He turned, pulled back in Fright and bumped into Sophie.

For rearing up on their hind Legs, their Wings splayed, Rogue-Bee and Pale-Bee were advancing Bee-Step by Bee-Step.

Pale-Bee stabbed the Air with her Stinger.

Sophie spread her Wings and reared up on her hind Legs to face Pale-Bee. The top of Sophie's Head turned shocking Blue.

Wil blocked Sophie's Path. *NOT SWEET!* he buzzed frantically.

XXXII The Plan Executed

Wings sparkling, as if it wished it could fly with its brothers and sisters...

NUNC AUT NUMQUAM.
NOW OR NEVER.

Wil pulled at Sophie's Wings. *Hide!* he buzzed.

Sophie shrugged Wil away; she stuck out her long Tongue at Pale-Bee and flexed her Stinger.

Pale-Bee swayed from side to side, her front Legs scraping the Air, while Rogue-Bee glared at Wil and lowered his Head, as if he were a maddened Bull about to charge.

Wil hunkered down to meet Rogue-Bee head on, his Bee-Heart pounding in his lower Abdomen. *Now or never, never surrender.*

The four Bees stared balefully at each other, surrounded by a great Ring of Thousands of Sister Bees and Brother Drones humming.

❖❖❖❖❖❖

The belly of the stone gargoyle seemed to sway and groan, and Portia and Portius moaned in their sleep.

❖❖❖❖❖❖

Beatriz and Phinneas ran across Gruffud's grounds just as the great glowing orb of the sun was rising majestically above the horizon in the East Field.

"It's your fault we're late," said Phinneas. He was feeling sleepless and thoroughly out of sorts. "We should have gotten here a lot earlier. If you hadn't spent half an hour eating breakfast—" But he didn't finish his sentence. Sometimes, Beatriz is a real pain, he thought.

"Everything is going according to your Big Plan, Phinn. We're here. The sun is here. We're only missing a couple of key people?" said Beatriz, her voice rising.

"Very funny," said Phinneas.

"Well, what do you suggest we do now?" asked Beatriz conversationally. "Why don't we…um…sit down on the flat rock over there and wait for Wil and Sophie to fly by. Yes, that's what we should do."

Not having any better proposal, Phinneas walked over to the rock and sat down. He pulled out the four crystals from his pocket. "You do have the dragonfly, don't you?" he asked.

"Fine time to check and make sure I didn't forget it. Of course, I've got it. The whole thing wouldn't work otherwise, would it?"

She pulled out the glass jar with the dead dragonfly in it from the bag she was carrying. Unscrewing the top of the jar, she carefully cradled the dead dragonfly in her hand and placed it on the rock in the sun. Its wings glistened in the sun's rays. She smiled.

"Okay," she said. "You hold two of the crystals up in the sunlight and I'll hold the other two up—"

"And we'll both say the words at the same time," said Phinneas, interrupting her. "Don't you think you're sounding a little bossy, by the way, given the fact this whole thing was my idea?"

"We won't close our eyes, okay?" said Beatriz, pointedly ignoring Phinneas's comment.

"No, definitely not," said Phinneas. "We don't want to miss anything this time."

"If anything actually happens, Phinn," said Beatriz.

"You could sound a little more positive and say when anything happens," said Phinn, but he didn't feel all that sure himself.

Holding the four crystals up so they would catch the sun's rays, they slowly chanted, *"Tawari, kamahi, manuka, pohutukawa."*

They gazed around expectantly and were both surprised to see a dozen dragonflies hovering above their heads.

"Where did those come from?" asked Phinneas.

"I wonder," said Beatriz thoughtfully. "Maybe the dead dragonfly is like a duck decoy—you know, other dragonflies see it and think the rock is a safe place."

Phinneas looked down at the dead dragonfly. Its wings were sparkling, as if it wished it could fly with its brothers and sisters.

A moment later, there was a sudden, sharp sound like an explosion.

"What was that?" asked Beatriz, her voice tense.

❖❖❖❖❖❖

The gargoyle lurched and with a mighty explosion, its stone belly burst apart. A tear rolled down Portia's left cheek and Portius bowed his head.

❖❖❖❖❖❖

In a frightening Flash, Sophie and Wil were thrown high into the Air inside the Scream of Thousands of Sister Bees and the Drones.

His Wings bent and Fur flat, Wil struggled to buzz his Wings. One of his Antennae dangled uselessly over his fifth Eye.

Portia and Portius were right. The Buzzroar of the Bees had been powerful enough to split Stone asunder.

Wil twisted his head, searching for Sophie, but couldn't see her anywhere.

Something tickled his Bee-Fur.

There she was, right above him, the Bee-Fur on top of her Head glowing blazing Yellow. She waggled her Antennae.

Saved, she buzzed, and in a mad Dash she zinged into the gaping Hole in the Stone. Wil followed her…

And there, he saw them. Pinned beneath a large Stone lay Pale-Bee and Rogue-Bee, both trapped. They stared up at Wil and Sophie, their Fur bristling. Pale-Bee clenched her Stinger.

❖❖❖❖❖❖

162

Phinneas pointed to the roof of the school. "Look, up there!"

Where there had been a stone gargoyle a moment before, now there was only a gaping stone with a large hole in it.

Beatriz and Phinneas watched in amazement as rubble from the gargoyle ricocheted to the ground. A small, trembling cloud rose up from the gaping stone and hovered in the air above the greenhouse.

✦✦✦✦✦✦

Throbbing, quivering, swirling, the Throng of jubilant Bees hovered above the Shining Comb. Swept along by the rustling of Thousands of beating Wings following Mother-of-Us-All, Sophie and Wil winged their way high into the Sky, swooping and diving. The Pull of the Sunlight on their Wings vanquished the last, lingering Vapours of the cold, black Cloud.

Freedom, buzzed thousands of Bees—they looked like Flying Jewels or Sparkling Raindrops. A scented Song of Triumph filled the Air.

> *Retribution Beneath the Sky,*
> *Lapsus Oculi, Leges Loci*
> *Marauder Vanquished, Marauders Die*
> *Mother-of-Us-All to our Next Palais*
> *Hurrah, Gaudeamus*
> *Hurray, Praise this Day!*

Sophie whooshed through the air in front of Wil, her Bee-Fur sparkling in the Dawn Light. Buzzing loudly, she taunted him, *Can't catch me.*

Oh yes, I can! retorted Wil and he darted after her, the Wind roaring through his Bee-Fur.

✦✦✦✦✦✦

"Do you see what I see?" asked Beatriz, squinting at the dark cloud.

"Bees," said Phinneas. "I told you so. Quick, hold up the crystals."

The crystals flashed and the dragonflies swooped in great circles around the children's heads. Small rainbows played in the air and on the ground.

163

✤✤✤✤✤✤

Breathless, Sophie and Wil caught up with the Throng of Bees as it headed to a Grove of Trees near the Hives, but shimmering Colours of Blue and Green and Yellow below them caught their Eyes.

Rainbows, buzzed Wil.

Shape-shift, Sophie replied. She dipped her Wings and drew a broad Circle back towards the Rainbows flashing in the Air.

Dragonflies, she buzzed.

Now or never, Wil buzzed back. He swooped high into the Sky followed closely by Sophie. With a last Gaze at the Sun and whooping like Banshees—*One for All and All for One*—they plunged so quickly that Wil's Bee-Breath was swept away. Blinded by four Flashes of bright Light, they swerved through the Dragonflies.

Rainbows brushed their Wings.

An instant later, Wil felt his Wings melt away. The voice of Mother-of-Us-All urging her Charges to Safety faded…

His legs became heavy, leaden like stone.

✤✤✤✤✤✤

Dropping out of the sky like two acorns falling from an oak tree, Sophie and Wil tumbled right onto the ground in front of Phinneas and Beatriz.

Phinneas and Beatriz stared at them, speechless.

Then Phinneas hollered, "Can you believe it? Bea, we did it! We did it!"

Beatriz ran around and around Wil and Sophie in circles, shrieking, "You're back! You're back!" She picked up Sophie's eyeglasses from the ground and handed them to her.

"Glad…t-t-to…see…you!" said Sophie, staggering to her knees. She put her glasses on and the frames turned a glorious red, as brilliant as Aurora's great glowing orb hanging above the horizon.

Wil was still splayed out on the ground. His legs refused to budge. He tried to move his lips but they felt rubbery, and his tongue felt stupid and thick. "Wait…wait until you hear…what happened to us!" he finally managed to blurt out.

XXXIII Future Fortunes

Two snakes coiled around the inkwell, gazing up longingly
at the green frog squatting on the lily pad lid.

MAGNUS CREPITANS SERPENS SERPTUS
IN ANGULUM SE GLOMERAVIT,
SED OMES ILLUM DISSIMULANT.
SEE…A BIG RATTLESNAKE IS COILED
IN THE CORNER OF THE ROOM.
BUT EVERYONE IS PRETENDING
IT REALLY ISN'T THERE.

"August 22nd—one day late, children. Happy Birthday, both of you," said Aunt Violet, smiling fondly at Wil and Sophie.

"Better late than never," said Aunt Rue, as she carried in Sophie's and Wil's birthday cake from the kitchen to the living room—the large cake in the shape of a dragonfly decorated with small shining silver balls. "Twenty-two candles—and an extra two to grow with!"

Sophie opened a box with a new feather quill pen from Aunt Violet and Aunt Rue, and an inkwell. Two snakes coiled around the inkwell, gazing up longingly at a green frog squatting on the lily pad lid.

"It's beautiful," said Sophie, clutching the pen tightly. "I think the first thing I'm going to draw is a picture of the queen bee. The bees call her Mother-of-Us-All, you know."

"Really?" said Aunt Rue, with an intense look of interest on her face.

Wil got an amazing new book from Aunt Rue and Aunt Violet— *The Big Book of Snakes*. It had hundreds of coloured illustrations and stories about different snakes from all over the world.

And Sophie had a really special present for him. She had somehow managed to mend one of the snowsnakes from the Winterlude Festival. The long red and black rod was already hanging on his bedroom wall above his bed. And she had seemed pleased with the bracelet he had made for her from some of the Narcisse snake bones he had found; she was wearing it around her wrist.

Beatriz gave Sophie a bottle of expensive *Sassie's* nail polish, which changed colour every few minutes.

And Phinneas gave a large, ruby red marble to Wil—it reminded Wil of the Perfect Products salesman and his case of crystal ball marbles. Wil and Sophie had never mentioned Aunt Violet's crystal ball escapade to Aunt Rue, just as they had promised.

"And before I forget," said Aunt Rue, "Mage Radix was kind enough to send along a huge jar of honey for us. Just regular honey," she said, laughing at the expression on the children's faces.

Wil had never had such a birthday celebration and couldn't believe his good fortune—delicious cake, presents, new friends, Rufus Crookshank gone once and for all. Even if the Serpent's Chain had returned—according to the prophecy in the Great Nest—it hardly seemed to matter tonight.

While Sophie, Wil, Beatriz and Phinneas were examining all the presents—and Cadmus was batting the red marble around on living room carpet—Mrs. Bain turned to Aunt Rue. "So, you think there's more to all this Serpent's Chain business than we're hearing in the newspapers? Is there some kind of cover-up going on?" she asked.

"I think the Secretariat is trying to ensure the media coverage is balanced," said Aunt Rue, obviously choosing her words carefully. "The Secretariat's position is that there is no need to alarm the general public. Still, there does seem to be no end of rumour."

"Rue...Rue...birthday celebrations are happy times," chided Aunt Violet from the kitchen, where she was pouring another batch of honey spice into a pitcher. "Don't be so dour. We don't need to worry about the Serpent's Chain, not tonight."

Mrs. Bain changed the subject quickly. "So, what are you working on, Aunt Violet?" she asked.

"Me?" asked Aunt Violet, looking startled. "Well, the garden keeps me busy. But I do have a small project underway. I haven't really discussed it with anyone yet."

"How exciting," said Mrs. Bain encouragingly, as she took another bite of cake. "Delicious," she murmured. "So, are you going to tell us what it's about?"

"Yes, well, it is fun," said Aunt Violet, sounding a little flustered. "Well, it's not *just* fun, of course. Obviously it's a business proposition and a business has to sustain itself."

Aunt Rue's expression at this news was comical, thought Wil. Her eyebrows were raised—the top half of her face looked surprised. But she was biting her bottom lip, and the bottom half looked slightly horrified.

"What's the project, Aunt Violet?" asked Sophie, tearing herself away from a picture of a black and white king snake swallowing a rattlesnake in *The Big Book of Snakes*.

"Well, I thought you knew already, children," said Aunt Violet. "You've been helping all year."

"We have?" asked Wil. Sophie looked as mystified as he felt—along with Aunt Rue. Aunt Violet had obviously not even spoken to Aunt Rue about her plans.

"I'm setting up a fortune-telling business," said Aunt Violet quietly, without looking at Aunt Rue.

"Why didn't you tell us?" asked Sophie.

"You never asked," said Aunt Violet brightly.

"What's the name of your business going to be?" asked Mrs. Bain.

"I don't really have one yet," said Aunt Violet. "But I have been thinking about something along the lines of *Over the Rainbow Fortunes or Happy Fortunes.*"

"But not all fortunes are happy," Wil pointed out.

"You're probably right," said Aunt Violet, "but do you honestly think anyone would want to visit a shop promising *Unhappy Fortunes?*

"What about *Auntie Vi's Fortune Telling?*" said Beatriz suddenly.

"That sounds good," said Aunt Rue out of the blue.

Aunt Violet looked surprised at Aunt Rue's endorsement, as if she had been sure that Aunt Rue was going to put her foot down and say, *Impossible! A fortune-telling business? What a scaly idea.*

"*Auntie Vi's Fortune Telling* does seem perfectly straight forward," said Mrs. Bain.

"It tells everyone exactly what to expect," said Phinneas.

"*Auntie Vi's Fortune Telling* it is," said Aunt Violet, with a look of glee on her face.

✦✦✦✦✦✦

Long after the birthday celebrations had ended...

Long after Aunt Rue had lit her nightly candle for Cyril Isidor in the kitchen window...

And long after Aunt Violet had finally shuffled off to bed, complaining—but looking rather pleased at the same time—that she'd had far too much excitement over the last two days, "enough to last anyone a snake's lifetime"...

Sophie and Wil finally had a chance to confer. They sat on the floor in Wil's bedroom whispering, Esme safely coiled around Wil's arm—for Wil had blocked up the hole in the floor with a thick wad of paper.

"We should have said something about the Serpent's Chain," asked Sophie.

"What and have everyone look at us like we're crazy?" said Wil. "You heard Aunt Rue. *The Secretariat's position is that there is no need to alarm the general public.* We're trying to help Aunt Rue keep her job, not have her get fired. Besides, we might have imagined it all. Maybe it was a hallucination from that black cloud. Or maybe Rufus Crookshank and Lucretia Daggar were trying to scare us, and they broadcast the words somehow," said Wil, but he knew those were lies.

Sophie shook her head. "You know that's not true."

Wil pulled out the black medallion—there were now two small figures outlined on the medallion. A serpent and a bee.

"I miss the bees," said Sophie, the frames of her glasses as dark as her eyes.

"Me too," said Wil simply. There was nothing more to say, he thought. The warmth of the Great Nest, the comforting smell of Mother-of-Us-All, the steady Order of the Honeycomb, the intoxication of *Sweet*, chasing the wind, *One for All and All for One*…all these, they would never forget.

Taking a breath, Sophie asked, "Do you think the medallion is going to send us on another task?"

Wil shrugged. "I don't know. Right now, I'm ready to go back to school, aren't you? Especially with Phinneas and Beatriz. And we don't have to worry about Rufus Crookshank and Lucretia Daggar any more. They're in the hands of the Firecatchers—for good."

"Maybe Aunt Rue will have a better time at work now with Lucretia Daggar gone," said Sophie.

"I hope so," said Wil. "Don't you think it's strange how Aunt Rue and Aunt Violet won't answer our questions sometimes? We don't even know when their birthdays are, for snake's sake."

"They probably don't want us to know how old they are," said Sophie with a grin.

"But you can't ignore something forever," said Wil. "Even if the Secretariat and everyone else acts as though the Serpent's Chain isn't real, they must be scared or they wouldn't have tried to hide the *magykalis* bees. We know the Serpent's Chain is back, and so do they—but it's like a big rattlesnake is coiled in the corner of the room, and everyone is pretending it really isn't there."

EPILOGUE

SI FINIS BONUS EST, TOTUM BONUM ERIT ANNON?
ALL'S WELL THAT ENDS WELL…OR IS IT?

Mage Radix brought out the old wicker skep in the storage shed. The colony of wild *apis mellifera magykalis* bees seemed pleased to take it up as their new residence, after having absconded from the belly of the gargoyle. Mage Radix returned not just one but two hives to the safe keeping of the Secretariat on the Status of Magical Creatures (S.S.M.C.) at the end of the summer.

Stone rubble (the sorry remains of the Gruffud's gargoyle) littered the Gruffud's lawns. Mage Radix ruefully inspected the fragments, hoping he could repair it, but the gargoyle had been truly smashed to smithereens.

An advertisement for an Assistant Deputy Minister—Lucretia Daggar's former position—was posted within seventeen working days by the S.S.M.C. Interested applicants were told the former Assistant Deputy Minister had *retired.*

An article the following month in *The Daily Magezine* brought to light the salacious fact that Lucretia Daggar and Rufus Crookshank had been cousins and secret lovers. Crookshank's return to MiddleGate had apparently re-kindled their affair; and according to unofficial reports, Daggar visited Crookshank in captivity the night he was first arrested. While the article hinted at Crookshank's and Daggar's purported links to the secret society known as the Serpent's Chain, the revival of the society—or indeed, the very idea that it had ever really existed—was dismissed by the author of the article. Others pooh-poohed the whole thing, grumbling it was all a government election ploy—as the elections were being called within the year.

For the time being, rumours about the revival of the Serpent's Chain seemed to have been quelled...

And the gargoyle in the backyard, by the way, seemed saddened to have Esme leave its company and return to Wil's good keep. Wil left three fresh quail eggs near the gargoyle, however, which seemed to restore it to better humour.

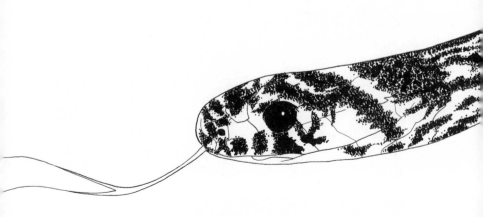